CRICKETS *On* COCAINE

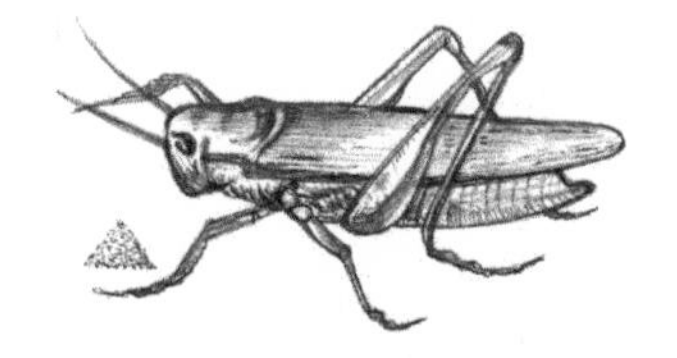

Interior design by Petya Tsankova

ISBN paperback: 978-1-9163708-0-7
ISBN ebook: 978-1-9163708-1-4

This paperback can be ordered through all bookstores and Amazon. The e-book is also obtainable from e-platforms such as Amazon and iBook, among others.
Also directly from Nettie at **nettiefirman@btinternet.com**

CRICKETS
On
COCAINE

For Sarah -
Thank you for buying my book,
which I hope you enjoy.

Nettie G.

NETTIE
FIRMAN

I am not a writer except when I write.

Juan Carlos Onetti

Turn your face into the sun and the shadows will fall behind you.

Maori Proverb

A stiff prick carries no conscience.

Angela Mead

TABLE OF CONTENTS

GOOD MANNERS 1994

For Bernard

On the last evening of the cruise, Lee and Debs invited Maurice Webb into their cabin. That was six months ago now, Maurice reflected, as he went into his spare room to make the finishing touches. He plucked a wilting petal off the single red amaryllis, which his mother-in-law had sent him for Christmas to grow from a bulb kit, and straightened the three tumblers on the teak side table.

Since he had lost his wife two years previously, his mother-in-law persisted in sending him presents with an activity theme, but as he only ever bought pre-planted window boxes, gardening was never going to become a hobby. He had other interests to cultivate now. Come to think of it, he had never even looked at the starter-pack magazine for collecting miniature models of classic cars either. Maurice was not interested in cars, only in the value of their number plates, although he did maintain his own car, keeping it protected under an expensive, fitted-plastic cover during the winter months on the concrete forecourt in front of his bungalow. A newly-purchased pampas grass, the only sign of vegetation, grew proudly erect from a metal-strapped wooden tub.

Not knowing whether they would be having the sandwiches first and the main meal later, he was undecided as to whether to leave any snacks out in the bedroom. Nuts made your mouth dry and lodged in your teeth, and crisps encouraged drinking. He had been to other people's houses, but never hosted, so it was a first for him and he felt slightly apprehensive.

The spare room with its French doors at the rear of his bungalow led onto a small, nondescript, decked garden with a brick barbeque and wooden shed. Flanked by similar bungalows, the area wasn't overlooked, but it being February they wouldn't be going outside anyway. Maurice considered all this while his guests were already half an hour late.

Having put the heating up to twenty-eight degrees to make the place welcoming, it now felt stiflingly hot and he changed into a short-sleeved shirt. He opened the hall and sitting room windows just enough not to let the drizzle in and settled down in his leather armchair with a can of lager and the Saturday Mail. The sitting room had been Pat's bedroom for the last year of her life, when they had moved into the bungalow for ease of care. A cinema-sized plasma screen now occupied the end of the room where Pat's special electric bed had been. Sometimes, towards the end, when her pads were overdue for changing, Pat believed that her air-bed had leaked water. Their daughter Sheila had been wonderful, sharing the care with Maurice and agency nurses at night. Neighbours from their old house visited frequently, bearing gossip and mashed monochrome meals, allowing Maurice to visit his snooker club for a couple of hours or go for a pint. They had had a good marriage of thirty-one years and he missed her and the white noise of daytime television: chat shows, soaps and reality tv, which kept Pat in touch with the outside world, something she'd never be part of again. He'd only been unfaithful to her once in their marriage with a lady he met at the pub when Pat had first become ill, and she and Sheila had gone on a weekend coach trip to the Isle of Wight to visit Osborne House and the Botanical Gardens at Ventnor. He was in need of some physical comfort and had amazed himself with his uninhibited and prolonged performance, and the blatant enjoyment it had obviously given his partner. He regularly relived the memories of that night and they occupied and grew in his fantasies, but had remained there, having mutually agreed not to keep in touch.

Maurice wondered what Jim and Sandra's surname was. Etiquette dictated first names only, rather like Alcoholics Anonymous, but being in the personalised number plate trade, he would dearly have liked to know as there could be a bit of business to be done as well. He had a JSC registration and a JD one, but the chances were slim of their surname beginning with a C or a D, even though they were common letters. It would be easy enough for Jim and Sandra to discover his own surname if they poked around, but all bills, post and paperwork had been put away and out of sight. Maurice kept the bungalow meticulously tidy and prided himself in knowing exactly where anything was at any given moment. It was becoming a slight obsession, particularly the cleanliness of the bathroom, and he hoped there wouldn't be too much to put straight, or at worst offend him, once his guests had gone. Such was the risk of home entertaining, but he consciously tried to put these negative thoughts aside and concentrate on the fun ahead.

There were rules and guidelines on every level in this

business: no talk of what you do for a living or attempting to discover a mutual friend or connection; the skeletal bones of how to socialise normally were thus removed. But there was still plenty to talk about. Only mobile phone numbers given, and no addresses exchanged until after the first meeting on neutral territory. And obviously, only if that had all gone well and they wanted to meet again for longer. It didn't always have to be weekends, but usually was. As he worked from home now, the days were all much the same, apart from Wednesday evenings at The Lodge and Friday mornings the supermarket.

Maurice fingered the small gold Egyptian scarab around his neck and thought about his Nile cruise the summer before. He'd gone with the intention of meeting new friends, or a particular friend, and his hopes had more than paid off. The cruise boat, with its capacity for a hundred passengers, had only forty guests that week due to the troubles in Cairo and the excessive August heat, and there were plenty of singles aboard. Despite his attempts, he didn't find a lady friend, but his life had opened up in a way he could not possibly have imagined. After dinner, the nights on deck were long, balmy and decadent. Small regular groups formed around the circular bamboo and glass tables, and strong bonds forged with the exchange of increasingly outrageous and exaggerated stories, fuelled by regular double gin and tonics served every twenty minutes until the waiters went off duty around midnight, leaving the hard core with a selection of drinks to keep them going. There was never any drunkenness, but perhaps that was due to the combination of guests on that particular week, or more likely that they were all seasoned drinkers. The feeling shared was one of complete happiness and personal abandonment and the belief that where they all were at that moment would last forever, encapsulated in their safe and small hedonistic world of comradeship and warmth, a million miles removed from their everyday lives.

He had since visited Lee and Debs twice at their flat in Wembley and with their help chose a cheeky user-name and got himself up and running on various swinging websites. Maurice's on-line profile gave little away about him, but the photographs he posted were impressive. The opportunities were endless, and surfing the many swinging sites took up a good deal of his time.

They were now over an hour late. His mobile rang. Jesus Christ – it was Sheila, wanting to come round immediately to fetch her ski suit from the spare room cupboard to lend to a friend. That was all he needed. The video machine and stack of explicit videos, the maroon sateen sheets bought especially for the occasion. He had to keep her away. Fuelled by panic and a sudden rush of adrenalin, he told her of his chronic diarrhoea and vomiting bug and successfully put her off. He poured himself a large vodka and tonic, took a chilled bottle of Pinot Grigio out of the fridge and put on Elton John's Love Songs.

The doorbell rang. Jim was fatter than he remembered and had a slight band of sweat across his forehead and droplets of it on his upper lip. Sandra also looked flushed and was dressed provocatively in a flimsy transparent black and white top, more suited to the beach, with tight black leather trousers and cowboy boots. But she looked great and Maurice felt a pleasing stir. She kissed him on the lips, grabbed his buttocks and pressed herself against him, gyrating her hips in an exaggerated way and Jim slapped him on the back. Maurice struggled to shut the door on them, slightly anxious that the neighbours might see. Before they were through the porch, Jim explained that their lateness was not due traffic on the M1, as Maurice had assumed, but because he needed to stop for a crap at a pub on the outskirts of Derby and Sandra wanted a drink. Five Bacardi and cokes later between them, they'd lost track of time. Jim belched and apologised. Too much information, Maurice thought, as he ushered them in. On one front he'd discovered, at the age of fifty-nine, the rampant sexual animal in himself, hidden all these years. But outside of that sphere, he was conventional and private.

Once their bag was in the spare room, the men left Sandra to freshen up while they took care of the parking arrangements. As he lived fairly centrally, there were restrictions all day on a Saturday so Maurice had made just enough room on his forecourt to accommodate them. He guided in their big, black Mercedes, noting with disappointment their number plate: JAS 69. They had a little joke about it, and Jim told Maurice with great pride and authority that it had cost him a lot of money. Meanwhile, Sandra had made herself well at home, poured a tumbler of white wine, changed the CD to Bruce Springsteen and pumped up the volume. She was lying on the settee looking at his and Pat's wedding album when they came in. Maurice immediately felt ill at ease and suddenly wished they hadn't come. He would never have helped himself to a drink or changed the music in someone else's house, let alone looked at their photographs, and considered it basic bad manners. He was going to have to make a big effort to disguise his discomfort.

He went into the kitchen to get Jim a beer, took a deep breath, and carried the plate of ham and cheese sandwiches through to his guests. Jim was looking at his collection of biographies and Sandra had refilled her glass, taken off her boots and was dancing around the living room, crooning with an imaginary microphone and trying to look seductive. Clearly now tipsy, she approached Maurice with her tongue flicking in and out of her mouth salaciously. The whole scene felt disgustingly contrived and wrong, and Maurice wondered how quickly he could get rid of them. He thought of Pat and her gentle, dying frailty in what was her bedroom, and felt acutely that she was watching over them. It all seemed disrespectful and downright sordid. He was not ready for home matches yet.

Sandra lit a cigarette.

That was it.

He asked them to leave.

Jim laughed and Sandra continued dancing while Maurice got their bag, slammed it down outside the front door and told them to get out. They looked rather puzzled, but realised there wasn't much point in staying as the guy was quite clearly a weirdo in his own environment.

Maurice heard Sandra call him "Wussey Webb" as he closed his front door, and worked out sometime later that the newspaper had given his surname away.

Never mind. There would be others. And at least he didn't have much clearing up to do.

LAXATIVES 2009

for Margaret

Eleanor had asked me to help her clear out her mother's house in preparation for renting it out, and boy, what stuff did she have: at least thirty pairs of glasses, thirty pairs of shoes, twenty-five handbags and tights – tights, tights, tights, mostly unopened. Wardrobes crammed with outfits, some still with their swinging tags; boxed silk scarves, pashminas in every shade, fur coats, cashmere cardigans, a ton of costume jewellery, classy bars of soaps and body unguents of every kind imaginable. And the cosmetics – vast quantities of hairsprays, body lotions, face wipes, toners, gift samples, shampoos, face-masks, conditioners, deodorants. Industrial quantities of cotton wool and packets of paracetemol and laxatives. A whole drawer of beautiful gifts, still immaculate in their packaging: letter-writing sets, leather keyrings, fountain pens, silk handkerchiefs, room-diffusers, candles, address books, purses, wallets, monogrammed hand-towels and flannels, unopened boxes of perfumes, expensive talcum powder, and all the paraphernalia that is not needed when you are eighty-two years old, but certainly would have been given with thought and love to Estelle over the years by her large family.

"Look at all this stuff, Ellie, and mostly new. Do you want to go through it?"

"No. It can all be chucked. I don't suppose Johnno or Yan-Yan would want anything."

"We can't chuck it. I'll take everything to the charity shop near my office if you like."

"Good idea."

I had no intention of doing that and would be selling it all on eBay, but keeping the soaps, cosmetics and medicines for our own use. Ellie was unobservant about that kind of thing.

As a social worker for the elderly, I knew it was not an easy decision to put a senior family member into a home, and often was the cause of sibling disputes: rifts over money, the type of accommodation needed, and the timing (sooner versus later). Sometimes, it was also dependent on the sale of a property to fund the care, but not in Estelle's case. Instead, there was a wicked and emotionally charged cocktail of guilt, greed, emotion and, of course, potential inheritance.

Estelle was becoming less aware of family frictions and plans. Her favourite son, Mark, had emigrated to New Zealand after qualifying as a doctor, and Ellie and I lived in Clerkenwell. Estelle was never reconciled to the fact that her daughter was a lesbian, but by the same token was proud to say that Ellie was an esteemed valuer of Chinese Nineteenth Century Art at Sotheby's. She always maintained that she wouldn't have minded if Mark or Johnno had been gay, which didn't make it any easier. She'd never liked me and wouldn't have been happy to know I was now rifling through her drawers and private possessions. I'd no idea that she was such a hoarder, but how could I have known? She'd been an elegant and organised lady, her house always tidy and uncluttered. It was like going through someone's stuff whom you didn't know.

Johnno, who lived nearest to Estelle, was a lawyer, and travelled frequently. A misogynist, he'd found his servile wife during a trip to Thailand, and I must say, Yan-Yan was a very dutiful and attentive daughter-in-law, sometimes summoned by Estelle in the middle of the night to clean up something untoward on account of forgetting how many laxatives she had taken. The eldest by six years, Johnno had never forgiven his parents for sending him away to boarding school – an unaffordable luxury for Mark and Eleanor. He had an insatiable appetite for sex, visiting prostitutes and escorts in London and regularly calling sex lines. His phone bill was astronomic. Yan-Yan asked no questions, nor made any sexual or other demands on him, uncomplaining in her role as unpaid housekeeper. Despite, or perhaps because of, being very rich, Johnno was against a top quality retirement home, so, following a majority decision with her executors, he had transferred the ownership of her house to the three siblings and taken control of her finances. Ellie had been outnumbered by her brothers on this matter, but she was used to that scenario. Estelle's current and only bank account stood at just under two thousand pounds. This being the sum of her declared assets, she was eligible for a council-funded home at a cost of just eighty-nine pounds a week, a huge saving of hundreds of pounds a month. Ellie was not happy with this choice, knowing her mother's tastes and expectations, but Johnno argued that with her advancing forgetfulness she would soon know no different. They had both taken Estelle for a Mental Health and Wellbeing Assessment at her local outpatients' clinic, where she was asked several diagnostic questions:

"How old are you, Mrs Harrington?" the young doctor enquired.

"If you look at the form in front of you, with my name on it, it will tell you."

Johnno had tried not to wince.

"And do you know what day of the week it is, Mrs Harrington?"

"Of course I don't," she'd snapped. "I'm not a weather forecaster."

"And do you know who the Prime Minister is, Mrs Harrington?"

"I forget that now, but if you need to know I am sure that my children will tell you. Why are you asking me all these stupid questions?"

"And could you count back from one hundred in sevens for me?"

No reply.

The doctor had lowered his head and wrote some notes.

Estelle was becoming increasingly and uncharacteristically aggressive, and by good chance had given an exemplary performance to Dr Cooper. Johnno was relieved.

"Mrs Harrington. Would you like to go with my nurse to have a nice cup of coffee?"

"I don't like coffee. Never have done. It gives you cancer, you know, but I would like a nice glass of sherry." Estelle, having been escorted to the tea bar by the nurse, left Dr Cooper with the opportunity to speak to Ellie and Johnno alone.

"I can see that your mother is fairly advanced with dementia. Probably of the frontal-lobe type. Is she often like this?"

"Oh, yes," Johnno assured the doctor, "most of the time now."

"And would you agree with this, Miss Harrington?"

Eleanor had bit her lip, knowing full well that she would not get her way with the more expensive care her mother (or Johnno) was fully able to afford, and lied. "Yes, I'm afraid so, Doctor."

"I understand that you are considering Sun Lodge as a potential home for Mrs. Harrington? I will therefore recommend to them by letter that your mother be given an assisted place there as soon as one is available. I'm afraid I don't know how long the current waiting list is."

"Only three, Dr Cooper. We've already been to look round," Johnno declared.

"I see. At this time of year we are probably talking weeks or at the most a couple of months."

Having Estelle in the car prevented Eleanor from telling Johnno what she thought of him, and they travelled in silence.

"Are you coming back to Johnno's for lunch, dear? Or perhaps I could take us all out?"

"No, Mummy, I'm sorry but I have to get back to town for a meeting this afternoon. I'll come and see you with Celia at the weekend, and maybe we could go out for lunch then."

"Have a safe journey," Estelle called out of the window, as Eleanor disappeared into Wimbledon underground station.

"Who was that man we were talking to, Johnno? He said he was a doctor, but he wasn't Dr. Peswani."

"No, Mother, Dr Peswani recommended that we go and see Dr. Cooper."

"Why?"

"Because we love you, Mother, and we want you to have the best care possible when you move into the Home."

"When am I going back home?"

"Mother. You're living with me and Yan-Yan until a place

comes up for you at Sun Lodge. We've discussed this many times before."

"But I don't want to live in Sun Lodge. I want to live at home."

Tired of these pointless conversations, Johnno was relieved to hand over his mother to Yan-Yan's care so that he could go to the Golf Club for a few drinks and play nine holes in the late autumn sunshine. Yan-Yan made Estelle some soup and settled her on the sofa in front of a television programme on antique-hunting, where she snoozed off until Johnno returned a few hours later.

"Hello, Mother. Have you had a good sleep?"

"I want to watch Teletubbies. Eh-oh. Where's Mark?"

"He's in New Zealand, but he'll be coming home for Christmas."

"To my home? Is it Christmas very soon?" The effects of the cream of cauliflower soup made Estelle fart loudly.

"That's better," she declared, as Johnno left the room in disgust.

In the kitchen he sounded off to his wife: "I can't take much more of her. She is getting worse by the day. It's alright for Mark and Ellie, but we are doing everything and I have really had enough. They have no idea what it's like having her here full time."

Yan-Yan soothed him by stroking his hair and pouring him a Scotch before he went into his study, slammed the door, and settled in front of his computer to watch porn.

Sooner than expected, and to Johnno's huge relief, a place became available at Sun Lodge five weeks later. There had been some sort of flu epidemic, which had knocked several of the inhabitants off their perches. I knew that state-funded nursing homes lost far more patients than private ones, who liked to preserve both their clientele and their reputations for the purpose of statistics.

Working in Haringey, I was pretty sure what to expect of Sun Lodge, but was pleasantly surprised when we visited Estelle for the first time the following Sunday. We found her sitting happily in the reception area, amongst her fellow residents, looking at a copy of Woman's Own.

"Hello, Estelle, you're looking very well and comfortable." I gave her a kiss and a small bunch of yellow roses.

"Hello, girls. What are you doing here? Have you come to visit someone?"

"Yes, Mummy, we've come to visit you!" Eleanor gushed with exaggerated enthusiasm.

"How did you know I was here? It is good timing because Johnno says I'm only staying for a few days before going back home." This was standard stuff.

"What's the food like, Mummy? Is it good?"

"Oh yes. We're having roast chicken, apple pie and ice cream for lunch."

"That sounds lovely, Mummy. Will you show us your room?"

Estelle rose slowly, and with the help of a stick guided us to the lift.

"Now, what floor am I on, dear? Two or three? I keep forgetting."

"You're on the second floor, Mummy."

Her room was compact, with a single cot-sided bed, teak wardrobe, small chest of drawers and an en-suite lavatory and basin. It overlooked a paved quadrangle with tables, chairs and planted raised beds. She had brought her own armchair and a few personal effects: photographs, a radio and a couple of paintings.

"This is very nice, Estelle," I said. "And you've a good-sized television."

"I can't work it, dear. Maybe you could show me."

Eleanor picked up the large-digit remote control.

"Mummy, this red button on the top right turns it on and off, and you press the numbers for what channel you want to watch. It's quite easy."

"Thank you, dear. Could you go and find a vase to put the flowers in?"

I offered to do this, it being an opportunity to snoop around.

The small lounge at the end of Estelle's corridor was also a food preparation area, where sandwiches, snacks and drinks were made. It smelt of rancid milk and urine. Residents sat round the edge of the room, some reading, some snoozing, some gazing vacantly, while a wide-screen television blasted out a game show at high volume. By the time I got back, Estelle looked cross and was agitatedly fiddling with the remote control, oblivious to my presence.

"Mummy," said Eleanor, rising from the bed, "we're so happy to see how well you've settled in, but we must be going now." The departing platitudes were ignored by Estelle, who was engrossed with the game show.

"Well, that went as smoothly as it could, didn't it, Cee? Mummy seems reasonably happy with everything, but let's just pop in to see Carole to get her version of things." Carole Richards was the manager of Sun Lodge, and her office was next to the front door. She was fairly brisk in her manner, but approachable and friendly, and I was impressed that she knew who we were immediately.

"Do please come in, Eleanor, and take a seat."

"Carole, this is Celia, my partner."

"How do you do, Celia. Have you seen Estelle yet?"

"Yes, we have, and we think she's settling in well. How do you think she's been?"

"It is early days, but she hasn't given us any concerns yet. She has a good appetite and loves her food, doesn't she?"

"She does indeed."

"We try to keep the food standards high at Sun Lodge. It's shocking how some homes feed their patients. Now, just a bit of housekeeping. Your brother said she wouldn't want a daily newspaper in her room, but there are always papers in the lounges and at reception. Also, most of our guests have a podiatry treatment every six weeks or so, at a cost of twelve pounds, from our visiting chiropodist. I don't think I mentioned this to your brother, but I would really recommend it as their feet do get swollen and dry in the warmth of the home."

"Yes, of course, Carole. That's fine, thank you."

"Also," Carole continued, "a hairdresser comes in twice a week to trim the gents or give them a shave, and give the ladies a wash and set, or cut, if necessary. She charges ten pounds for the ladies, without a cut."

"Again, that is fine, Carole. Maybe Mummy could be done twice a month."

"I'll arrange that on Monday. It does so lift their spirits when their hair looks nice. Well, it does for all of us, doesn't it, ladies? Finally, I don't know if you saw that we have a small shop next to the dining room, selling confectionery, toiletries, greeting cards, stationery, stamps and so on. It gives our guests a feeling of independence to do a bit of their own shopping, and most of them are given ten pounds a week from their cash float, which I keep here in the safe. It really is more than enough, and your brother has deposited two hundred and fifty pounds with me, which will keep your mother going for several months. We do ask for cash rather than cheques as it would all get rather complicated with over fifty residents. Also, we don't allow our residents to have mobile phones. I don't know if your brother told you? They are intrusive to others, and calls are often not terminated properly, resulting in large bills. We have a mobile telephone unit on each floor, which can be wheeled into bedrooms, and most of the patients are issued with a card, which again gets topped up by cash, and deducts credit when calls are made. Obviously it's free to receive calls. Your brother has put forty pounds onto your mother's phone card. I think that covers just about everything. Our telephone is manned twenty-four hours a day and we are always here if you have any concerns whatsoever. I'm sorry about all these details and taking up your time, but we want Estelle to have the best care that we offer to all our residents."

"Thank you so much, Carole. We feel that Mummy is in very good hands. We both live and work in London, but will try to visit as often as possible. Do you have my mobile number?"

"I do. Well, lovely to see you again, and to meet you, Celia."

In the car park, Ellie lit a cigarette and fumed. "Johnno told me nothing about all these things, and, knowing him, he will be sparing with the cash, but I like Carole and would think she runs a pretty tight ship. I think we have actually struck gold with this place."

It was also a huge relief to Johnno that Estelle had settled in so well at Sun Lodge, and the option of a more upmarket home was soon forgotten about. He ensured that the investments made with his mother's money were highly complicated and yielded him a certain amount of personal income, of which Eleanor and Mark were completely unaware. He was totally unscrupulous, and the tenants he had found for Estelle's house paid him an extra £200 each month in cash, which he told his siblings was for Yan-Yan to do the cleaning.

The next time we visited Estelle she was chatting to a distinguished-looking gentleman in the Reception area, having had her hair done, looking very happy and ten years younger.

"Mummy, how pretty you look. They've done your hair beautifully," Ellie enthused.

"Oh, hello girls. This is Siggy. He's Polish."

Siggy stood up and kissed our hands. As he bowed, his baggy trousers revealed an incontinence pad, and long, straggly chest hair poked through a missing button on his shirt.

"Good afternoon, ladies. How lovely to meet you. Can I get you a drink from the machine, which does cappuccino or espresso, hot chocolate or tea?"

"That would be very kind. Thank you. We both take espressos," I said, handing Estelle a box of chocolates. Siggy had thick, grey hair, swept back off his high forehead, and must have been very handsome in his youth. Returning with our coffees he announced:

"Your mother and I want to get married in the New Year, don't we, Piekna?"

"What?" Ellie exclaimed. "Does Johnno know of this plan, Mummy?" she enquired.

"What the devil has it got to do with him? Siggy invented the radio, and he's from Polish aristocracy."

"Not the radio, Piekna, that was Marconi. The video." We later learned that Siggy believed himself to be Ralph H. Baer, the German-born American Jewish inventor, who had developed early electronic games.

"Piekna means beautiful in Polish, you know," Estelle added.

The outlandish and unpredictable conversation was proving challenging, and I attempted to get back on to normal footing.

"Isn't it a beautiful Christmas tree?" I pointed to the hideously over-decorated edifice with flashing blue lights.

"It isn't real, dear."

"No, but it's very festive."

"Do you think so? I find it rather common."

Moving on, Ellie said, "Mummy, Mark is coming home for Christmas. It's only two weeks away. He'll be staying with Johnno and Yan-Yan and will then visit friends around the country. Isn't that exciting?"

"Not really. Tell him not to bother to come and see me. Siggy says that Christmas Day is very nice here. Carol singers come and Gordon dresses up as Father Christmas. Everyone gets a present and we have crackers with lunch." Ellie took Estelle's hand.

"Mummy, we really should be off now before it gets dark as we've seen a sign nearby where you can dig up your own Christmas tree, which we've always wanted to do."

"I wouldn't do that if I was you. Real trees drop a lot of needles you know, dear." The conversation, stilted as ever, was proving difficult and it was time to go.

After our goodbyes, Ellie lit her routine cigarette in the car park.

"Bloody hell. What on earth is going on there? They can't be serious about getting married. Do you think we should go back and speak to Carole?"

"No, I'm sure she's well aware of the situation," I said, "but I think you should discuss it with Johnno. I'm sure it's quite harmless and your mother did seem less confused and agitated. It's not unusual for attachments to be formed in old people's homes, and what harm can be done if it makes your Mum happy? I'm sure that the staff keep a close eye on these things."

"She's only been there a few weeks, but having said that if her friendship with Siggy develops in the next few months maybe they could pool their resources and move in to a better care home and share a little apartment. Anyway, I don't want to deal with it now or speak to Johnno. I'll call him later. Let's go."

"Let's not jump the gun, Ellie. You know that Johnno wouldn't want to spend any more money."

Estelle had been saving her weekly ten pound allowance, and had, by way of a five pound bribe, persuaded a young black carer called Precious to buy her a bottle of gin and eight boxes of laxatives. This was standard practice. She didn't like being constipated and, despite nightly requests, the occasional issue of a single laxative was not sufficient. She hid the booty in the pockets of her raincoat in the wardrobe, where she also cunningly disposed of the empty packets.

Some days later, valued Chinese clients were staying at the block of flats, owned by and opposite Sotheby's in Bond Streeet for the forthcoming auction. As was customary, Eleanor was taking them out for lunch in Mayfair the day before the sale when her mobile rang. It was Carole. "Eleanor, hello. I need to speak to you about your mother. Is it a good moment?" Eleanor excused herself and took the call outside the restaurant.

"We're having some issues with your mother on account of her loose stools and the sudden change in bowel habit, which has been going on for a few days now. It is not unusual for old people to get bouts of diarrhoea, we're quite used to that, but hers is very virulent and no other patient is affected. We've been giving her Imodium, but that doesn't seem to be helping. She saw the doctor this morning and has no temperature and still a good appetite. Has she ever been screened for bowel cancer, as it may be that she needs to have a colonoscopy? The doctor has recommended having blood tests done next week. Also, she is having to wear double incontinence pads now and that's not going down well. She keeps pulling them off."

Ellie was not au-fait with her mother's bowel habits, nor did she wish to be, but recalled that Yan-Yan had mentioned similar episodes. "I think she's prone to having a sensitive stomach and, as far as I know, she's never had any investigations. Have you spoken to my brother about this?"

"No, not yet, Eleanor. I thought it was more of a matter to discuss with you first, being her daughter. Men don't tend to deal very well with these sorts of things."

"Yes, I know. Well, thank you for ringing me, Carole. I'm sure you'll keep a close eye on her and maybe we can speak again tomorrow."

"Of course, Eleanor. Thank you. Goodbye now."

Later that afternoon Estelle rang Ellie for the first time.

"Dear, can you come and see me now. Something bad has happened."

"Mummy, what's happened?"

"A man has touched me down below."

"Oh, Mummy, was it Siggy?"

"No, a carer."

"A carer? Are you sure? Tell me what he did."

"Well, dear, I had a bath, and he washed me inappropriately at the back end."

"Mummy, how awful. Have you told anyone about this?"

"No, dear, but I think they're trying to poison me too."

"I'm quite sure that they're not, Mummy, but I'll come up this evening as soon as I've finished work."

"Don't bring Celia. Also, Siggy found a hedgehog in the car park today."

"I'll see you later, Mummy. Get some rest now and try not to worry."

Ellie rang me from her cab when she was on her way home. I was on eBay checking the bids for Estelle's stuff and had already made two hundred pounds.

"Cee, I have to go to Sun Lodge right away. Mummy says she's been touched inappropriately. Can you come with me."

"Oh my God, of course," I said, "Was it Siggy?"

"Apparently not – a male carer. We'll have to drive up as soon as I'm back."

On the journey, I tried to reassure Ellie that I had come across this scenario before. "I'm afraid it is a fact that some young, usually gay, men are sexually attracted to old ladies. Working in a nursing home is easy pickings, although they usually choose those who are not capable of making a complaint."

"That's disgusting, Cee. I think we should see Carole first, don't you?"

"Go carefully, Ellie. Your mother may have exaggerated the facts."

Carole was on the phone when we arrived, and gestured us to sit down.

"Good evening, ladies. Sorry about that. Funnily enough I was just about to ring you, Eleanor, because your mother has had another bad bout of diarrhoea. This time it happened in the upstairs lounge at teatime. I believe she was given a bath and has now gone to bed. Since I spoke to you earlier, I've been off duty to attend a funeral, so I haven't seen her yet myself."

"Carole," said Ellie authoritatively, "my mother has rung me to say she was inappropriately touched by one of your male carers whilst being bathed. I realise this is a serious allegation, but it needs to be addressed immediately."

Carole's face paled.

"I'm afraid this must be a fabrication on your mother's part, Eleanor. I've never heard of such a complaint here. You know she's prone to some fanciful ideas. She believes that Siggy has proposed to her."

"I know. That's something else I wish to talk to you about, but not now. Who was the carer who bathed Mummy?"

"Let me see. It would have been either Marshall or Gordon."

"And have there been any allegations before against Marshall or Gordon?"

Carole became defensive and crossed her arms tightly. "Of course not. I know everything that goes on here and this sort of thing is quite unheard of, I can assure you."

I had to interject at this point.

"If I may interrupt you, Carole. I'm a social worker for the elderly in north London, and it is not unheard of for gay male carers to molest old ladies."

"With respect, Celia. I think this is a private matter between Eleanor and myself, if you don't mind. What may go on wherever you work certainly does not go on here. I'll make my investigations tomorrow, Eleanor, and get back to you. Marshall and Gordon are now off duty for the night, but I would like to reassure you that I'm quite certain that these accusations are totally unfounded."

We were shown the door. To both our relief, Estelle was fast asleep.

"I'm afraid you're on a losing wicket there," I told Ellie on the drive home. "Carole was very guarded, but then she would be. It's a complicated issue when patients with dementia make such complaints. Depending on what she comes up with tomorrow we do have further options: I believe that Sun Lodge is owned by Redhouse Homes, which are known to me. Also there is always 'Safeguarding', a free service for anyone – young or elderly – who is under suspicion of being bullied, mistreated or abused. In fact, 'The Safeguarding Vulnerable Groups Act' has just been updated and passed by Parliament, which I can always remind Carole about. She won't like that, or a potential law suit, or the threat of involving the press, which I would be quite happy to mention too. That would put the frighteners on her."

"We can't do that, Cee. I just don't know what to make of it. Do you think Mummy was telling the truth? At the risk of sounding selfish, it's happening the night before one of our biggest auctions of the year."

"Let's go out for a burger and a bottle or two of red. Good idea?"

"Go for it."

The following morning, Carole's call was well timed when Eleanor was having a quick cigarette break discreetly around the corner from Sotheby's in Bond Street.

"Good Morning, Eleanor. I hope I've called at a good time." She'd cleared her throat. "I've made my investigations and spoken to Marshall, who bathed your mother yesterday afternoon. Without being indelicate, I am sure you will understand that by the nature of the washing required, it had to be in-depth, but was not indecent, and a flannel was used. He was completely mortified to think that your mother thought he had abused her, as this was absolutely not the case, I can assure you. Marshall would be happy to speak to you in person now. He's outside my office."

It made sense.

"No, I'd rather speak to him face-to-face, but thank you

for getting back to me. How's Mummy today?"

"She seems well and ate a full cooked breakfast. Her tummy seems to have settled down now, thankfully."

"Oh, that's good, Carole. I'll come up at the weekend and speak to Marshall then."

"Of course. He's on duty from Saturday afternoon until Sunday lunchtime, and I'm here until Sunday tea-time. Goodbye for now, Eleanor, and I hope I've reassured you."

"So, you've been placated to some extent by Carole?" I asked Ellie as we ate at a local Sushi bar that evening. "As I've told you, some people go into the care industry because their victims are easy pickings, particularly if they are sedated. This is normal practice after a complaint has been made, but there's nothing to prove yet. Let's see how the land lies at the weekend."

The following Sunday morning we drove up to Sun Lodge. It was three days before Christmas and very cold. Estelle was in her room, dressed and lying on the bed. She looked dazed.

"Mummy, hello."

No response. Estelle moaned.

"Mummy – are you O.K?"

"No, I'm not. Siggy's gone to hospital."

"Oh, Mummy, how dreadful. What's happened to him?"

"I don't know. They wouldn't tell me, but we'll still get married when he's better. The hedgehog is in a shoe box in his chest of drawers."

"I'll tell Carole about that, Mummy. Don't worry. Would you like to get up and come out for lunch with us?"

"No thank you, dear. I'm quite happy here and it's roast pork for lunch. I want to stay at home. It's very cold outside." No mention was made of the complaint which we had come to investigate, and we didn't bring the subject up.

Carole was bright and breezy as we entered her office.

"Good morning, ladies. Have you seen your mother yet?"

"Yes," Ellie replied. "She was very quiet and doesn't want to come out for lunch with us."

"No. She's been upset about Siggy. He caused a small fire in his bedroom by trying to dismantle his television and burnt his hand quite badly, nearly causing a fire. We've had to remove him permanently from Sun Lodge, which of course your mother isn't yet aware of. However, I think we've solved the tummy problems. When looking for something in your mother's wardrobe this morning one of our carers found five empty packets of laxatives in the pockets of her raincoat. So at least there's no need for colonic investigations, which is a relief."

"That's good, Carole, but where did she get all those laxatives from? Are they sold in the shop?"

"Oh no. No over-the-counter medication is sold in the shop. I expect she brought them in when she arrived, although that should have been checked on."

As the weeks passed, Estelle became more and more distant and not capable of ordering supplies from Precious, but she was content. We were relieved, and the only nuptials to take place in the Spring were between Ellie and myself. We moved in to Estelle's house in the summer as Johnno couldn't be bothered to deal with more tiresome tenants, so he let us have it for a song as a wedding present. He didn't attend our wedding as he was visiting Mark in New Zealand, but he gave us a lovely gift of an antique silver canteen of cutlery from Mappin & Webb. It was in immaculate condition, but as the knife handles were ivory I suggested that we sell it on eBay, which helped towards the cost of our honeymoon.

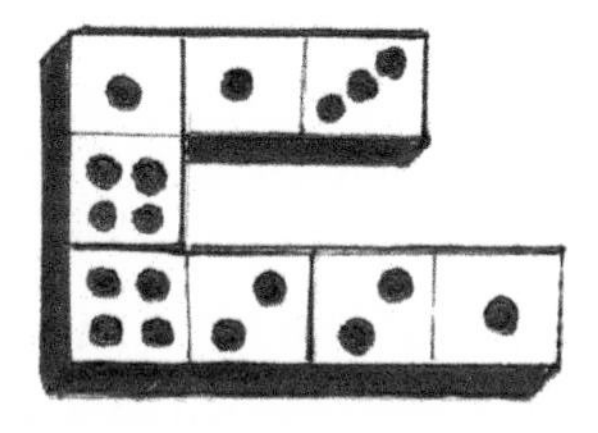

PARLOUR GAMES 1977

for Max

Closed down in the early 1980s, the school had been converted into retirement flats and duplexes. The main block, now extended with two extra wings, housed twelve apartments, and a board outside the Gate Lodge advertised: 'Poplar Place, Bespoke Accommodation for the Over-Sixties.'

The drive was the same, although the elms had been replaced by poplars, and the demolished riding stables were now a car park and utility area. Edward felt no emotion, merely curiosity, as he drove behind the main building and up the now tarmac-covered track to Mr Saunders' cottage. A lady was gardening in the front, and a man snoozing in a deck chair on the lawn. Impulsively, he decided to pull up and drop in.

"Good afternoon. My name's Edward Crawley. I'm so sorry to call in unannounced, but I attended Elm Park when it was a school, many moons ago. As my parents lived abroad, I spent many happy weekends and half terms in Elm Cottage, staying with Clive Saunders. I was in the area and thought I'd visit for old times' sake."

"How fascinating, Mr Crawley. Do please join me and my husband for some tea in the garden." She gestured for Edward to sit down and introductions were made.

"Peter, wake up, we have a visitor. This is Mr Crawley. He used to stay here as a boy."

The garden was more cared for and planted out than he remembered, but the cottage looked much the same. He hoped that they might invite him inside so he could see what they had done with it too; he could remember the layout exactly.

"How do you do. I understand you were at Elm Park? We had another chap call in here a few years ago by the name of Adrian – can't remember his surname – who also wanted to re-visit his childhood haunts. Did you know him?"

"I remember the name, but he was before my time." Edward was already feeling uncomfortable.

"I must say, he had some rum tales to tell. My goodness, what goings-on there were. It's hardly surprising that the school was shut down. Of course, many of those sorts of allegations are very popular with the press now. Look at Jimmy Savile, abusing his trusted position with those poor sick children. Disgusting. These ruddy people should be publicly castrated," he belligerently continued. "I hope nothing bad happened to you?" Edward blushed and wished he wasn't there. He wondered what sort of information Adrian had imparted.

"No, on the contrary, my time there was very happy, as was my brother's, and I was never aware of anything untoward."

"Rumour has it, doesn't it Julia, that Iain Catchpole went to stay with his sister in Devon, where he committed suicide before it came to trial. I believe his wife died shortly after." An awkward silence followed, and after some routine chat about life at Poplar Park, he made his excuses and left. He had gained nothing from the visit and regretted acting on a foolish impulse. Totally out of character for him. Edward had never quite come to terms with what had happened to him at prep school. Returning as a bachelor some forty years later, he had hoped to lay the memories to rest.

He stopped at the nearest pub to down a much-needed brandy.

*****

Situated just south of Hungerford, the boys called the school 'Diseased Park' on account of Dutch Elm disease which gradually ravaged the avenue of elms leading up to Elm Park in the 1970s. Founded after the First World War for sons of lost servicemen, it was still a small boys' preparatory school, accommodating just under a hundred pupils aged between seven and thirteen. Many of the boys' parents were in the services, and the school had a good reputation for being rounded, happy and healthy, although not highly academic.

Iain Catchpole and his wife, Esme, ran Elm Park in a relaxed manner, living in a flat in the main building where, as Headmaster, his study doubled-up as the Sixth-Form Common Room, a tradition introduced by the School's founder, the first Mr Catchpole. The more permissively minded parents thought it a good transition for the boys to make in their final year, learning consideration and, to a certain extent, tidiness. A ping-pong table occupied the bay window and two worn, large leather sofas and matching armchairs surrounded low tables where the boys played cards or games – Scrabble, Monopoly, Connect-4, dominoes, cribbage. The only rules being no dirty boots, balls or swearing, and the piano could be played – anything but scales, arpeggios or chopsticks. Curiously, the arrangement worked well and was not abused. As a sixth-form perk, the 'Grovers' (or 'Groovers' as they called themselves) also had their own small television room for organised viewing after supper during the week and on Saturday and Sunday afternoons, the Study/Common Room being out of bounds after supper.

Elm Park ticked along in its old-fashioned way. Most of the teachers were unqualified, their qualification being that they had themselves attended the school, or similar ones, and their calling was one of nostalgia and comfort. There had only ever been one school inspection, when the visiting inspector had watched a cricket match and then enjoyed several gin and tonics on the top lawn terrace with the headmaster and his wife, with no classroom looked at, nor examples of boys' work discussed.

Mr Catchpole was munificent, jovial and popular with both boys and parents. Elm Park had been a huge part of his life, where he was born, brought up and educated before attending Stowe and then Oxford. He returned as resident English master, living in a school cottage for ten years, and had married Esme, daughter of the then headmaster. So it was a natural rite of passage that he should follow in his father-in-law's footsteps at the age of thirty-five. Corpulent, with thick hair verging on ginger, and a red, puffy complexion, he always sported a bow tie. Photographs of his hideous, fleshy children graced his leather desk. Now approaching fifty, he made it his business to know every boy like the back of his hand, determined that their education be rounded, fun and memorable, if slightly eccentric. His headship came at a time when all this was achievable, and his son, Donald, had gone through the school without being bullied, despite often wearing an eye patch, having aggressive eczema and the fact of his father's position. It was a happy establishment and a blind eye was turned to cricket balls being bowled down the long corridors during the winter months, although there were always a lot of broken light bulbs to replace. The porter, responsible for general maintenance and for the handling and storage of trunks, kept four ponies, and the boys were encouraged to ride them bareback from their field to their stables in the evenings. They looked after them at weekends by way of cleaning tack, grooming and mucking-out, to be rewarded by hacks out along the abundant bridleways. Corporal punishment, although not yet banned, simply did not exist for breaking bounds or any other offence, and the tightly knit community and remoteness of the school excused contraband of cigarettes and alcohol. Mr Catchpole, himself being a smoker of cheroots, turned a blind eye to the occasional waft of cigarette smoke after an exeat or half term.

It was the summer of 1977 and Mr Catchpole's favourite term: cricket matches, paper chases, treasure hunts, nature rambles, Sports Day and more. Having sat their Common Entrance papers early in the spring term, it was a time to which the sixth-form boys would look back with longing and the realisation that it had been the most carefree summer of their lives and probably marked the end of their childhood, not that they would appreciate it at the time.

Mr Saunders (Geography) especially looked forward to seeing Edward Crawley again and to the prospect of having him staying in his cottage during the two exeats and half term. Well before Edward knew what 'perverted' meant, the older boys had enlightened him and he was mocked for being 'chosen' by Mr Saunders, but to Edward their friendship was a harmless privilege. He sometimes found sweets left under his pillow, and although missing his parents, he enjoyed staying at Mr Saunders' cottage, going to the cinema and being taken to watch local cricket matches, whilst his friends were at home with their parents or guardians. Small for his age, not sporty and rather reclusive,

Edward was highly intelligent and the only boy that year to have taken full scholarship papers. He had not been granted the status of prefect because he was too introverted and with no powers of leadership. His parents were posted to Cyprus, where his father, the youngest general in the British Army, commanded the military base in Akrotiri. His mother was very beautiful, and her extravagant hats, worn to the annual Garden Party, were a reliable source of embarrassment.

The term had started, and whilst the younger boys were being put to bed by Matron and the sixth formers catching up in their television room, Mr and Mrs Catchpole entertained four new parents for drinks in his study. At half past eight, Mr Catchpole summoned the Head Boy and prefects.

"Good evening Grovers. Welcome back and I hope you all had a good holiday. Could Connors, Gilbert, Hemsworth, Sanderson and Taylor please come along to my study now for our beginning of term Prefects' Meeting. I have an important announcement to make."

Assembled in the study, the boys were given a small glass of sherry by Mrs Catchpole after they had sung the first verse of the School Song, accompanied by her on the small grand piano. Mr Catchpole was flushed and looked excited as he gestured for the boys to be seated, whilst taking a large swig from his tumbler of whisky and lighting a cheroot.

"Now, Grovers, this is your final term at Elm Park and I want you to enjoy every moment and hold its sacred and fragrant memories in your hearts forever. I can promise you that the smells of roses and mown grass, summer sports of tennis and cricket, match teas and everything that the term promises will never be forgotten, culminating in the last night of term's epic picnic, where the band of The Royal Marines will be playing on the lower lawn. And this term you will get to belong to an exclusive club, like none other."

He had the boys' attention.

"This Club is, and always has been, the best kept secret of mine, my lady wife and all the previous Head Boys and Prefects of Elm Park. It was introduced by my late father, a keen thespian, in 1920 when the school was founded, so is a tradition of some fifty-seven years. I should perhaps mention that it was disbanded during the twelve years Headship of my predecessor, Mr Faraday, but I reinstated it in 1962 in memory of my father. It is called 'The Cloaca Club' and you are esteemed to belong to it. The only condition of membership is that the activities of Cloaca will never go beyond this room. We have some distinguished alumni: Quentin Crisp, Ian Fleming and Peter Cook to mention just a few. They have all gone on to have outstanding careers, and should be an inspiration to you all. Every member is expected to make a spirited contribution to our meetings."

A tatty leather Bible was produced and each boy in turn with his left hand on the bible and his right hand touching his heart was solemnly sworn in to the allegiance, commitment, secrecy and membership of The Cloaca Club.

"Well done, Grovers, and welcome to our theatrical Club. Does anyone know what Cloaca means?"

The boys looked vacant.

"C.L.O.A.C.A. It's a Latin word and I shall expect each and every one of you to know its meaning when we meet for our first soirée, a week on Friday. We assemble every two weeks and always have a theme in advance. The first one will be limericks invented by you on the subject of teachers or new boys. Is this quite clear?"

The boys smiled and nodded.

They liked the sound of the clandestine club, which they had been cajoled and seduced into joining, and approved of the potentially risqué subject for their first meeting. Mr Catchpole held open the heavy oak door of his study.

"Good night now, Grovers, and I am sure we are all looking forward to enjoying the fun and fruits of our select Club. Please be prompt at eight o'clock."

The ten days passed quickly and the meeting was greatly anticipated.

"Good evening, Grovers, and welcome to our first gathering. Please be seated."

Mrs Catchpole handed round weak lemon squash and bowls of Twiglets and crisps.

Mr Catchpole continued. "By tradition, our Head Boy will read out his dictionary definition of the meaning of our Club. Please, Hemsworth, the floor is yours."

Hemsworth cleared his throat.

"Thank you, Sir. From The Oxford Dictionary. 'The cloaca is a common cavity at the end of the digestive tract for the release of excretory and genital products in vertebrates (except most mammals) and certain invertebrates'."

"Well researched, Hemsworth, but I will now add the Chambers Dictionary definition. 'The terminal part of the gut into which urinary and reproductive ducts open, forming a single posterior opening; a sewer; a privy; a sink of moral filth'." The boys sniggered.

"Now, Grovers, which one do you prefer?"

There was no choice; it had to be the Headmaster's rendition.

"Excellent. Now we know what our Club is all about, can any of you please tell me one animal which has a cloaca?"

"A chicken, Sir."

"Correct, Gilbert."

"Sir," enquired Taylor, "does Matron have a cloaca?"

"Very good question, Taylor, and in truth I do not know, but I would think it highly unlikely. But I commend your contribution, which is exactly what is expected of our exclusive Members between these four walls - witty, but not offensive. Now, our opening theme this evening, as you know, is one of limericks, and may I invite Sanderson to be the first to entertain us."

Sanderson rose to the occasion:

"There was once a young chap named Knight
Who was so homesick he cried every night,
His tears, fat and sweet,
He wept onto his sheet,
And his teddy was bleached nearly white."

"That's a good limerick, Sanderson, but you cannot have two words sounding the same, even if the spelling's different."

"Yes, Sir."

"Next: Taylor."

"There once was a boy christened Piers
Who was bullied on account of large ears.
It made him so ill at ease
When his friends used to tease:
We will cut them both off with some shears."

"Very funny, Taylor Major, but I don't believe that Piers has in point of fact got large ears. Nevertheless, limericks don't have to be truthful." He took another large swig of his whisky. "And also, Taylor, the use of Christian names is not encouraged."

"No, Sir."

"Next, Connors, when you are ready."

"Sir, as there are only two new boys this term, I've come up with a limerick about Mr Hales."

"Very well. Go ahead."

"There was once a teacher named Hales
Who couldn't stop biting his nails,
He bit them so bad
All that he had
Were nailbeds resembling scales."

"Excellent, Connors, and truthful too! This has been a most satisfactory first meeting and I'm proud of you for entering into the spirit, but I fear we are running out of time. Our next theme is one of imitation – boys, teachers, parents, obviously exempting Mrs Catchpole and myself, and you may bring props."

A fortnight later they assembled again. Squash and nibbles were duly dispatched and Mr Catchpole clapped his hands together. "Welcome back, boys. Let us start with Gilbert tonight."

Gilbert stood up, without props, but was sucking his thumb. "It is a thame that thweet Thamuels can't thpeak properly."

With instant recognition, the boys clapped and Hemsworth responded, "Do you think that thweet Thamuels can thpell properly?"

Connors: "Do you think that thweet Thamuels can pissth properly?"

"Enough," barked Mr Catchpole, banging his gavel on the desk – a homage to his brief career as an auctioneer. "I think we all know of young Samuels' affliction with his lisp, but with speech therapy it can be improved. I do not approve of bullying on account of physical disabilities, as you know. Now, moving on. Taylor, I see you have brought along a bowl of fruit. Please commence."

Taylor placed the basket of fruit on his head and stuffed two rolls of socks from his pocket down the front of his shirt, approaching Mr Catchpole. "Good afternoon, Headmaster.

Lovely day for the Garden Party. Might I enquire why Edward has not been made a prefect in his final year next term? He is a hard-working and conscientious boy, and General Crawley and I would like him to follow in his brother's footsteps. We've been paying fees here now for some nine years and I hope you can give me a satisfactory explanation?" The boys clapped.

Next to take the stage was Connors, with a camp voice, and on the same theme. "Oh, Edward, how lovely it is to have you back at the cottage," he enthused. "We have a lot of treats in store this half term – swimming in flagrante, a trip to the cinema, where we will hold hands..."

"Stop now, Connors," said Mr Catchpole, thumping his gavel with great force. "Mr Saunders has looked after boys whose parents are abroad and has done so very well and given them a fine time. I'm quite sure that there are no goings-on like that. This Club may be avant-garde, but fundamentally it is decent and I will not tolerate such insinuations."

Connors made a mental note that Mr Catchpole's loose boundaries were somewhat hard to grasp.

"Our next theme, the last before half term," concluded Mr Catchpole, "will be dressing up as a girl or lady's character from children's literature. You must do your research carefully and may obtain full costumes and props from Mrs Elliot in the drama department. Goodnight boys."

Much fun was derived from selecting their muses and Mrs Elliot found outfits for them all. Connors grabbed a violin bow from the shelf of musical instruments and poked it under Sanderson's skirt.

"Does Dorothy have a cloaca? Let's have a look, chaps. My God! Yes she does!"

"How disgusting! Get that torch. I wondered what the pong

was!" Taylor picked up a trumpet and started to play John Stanley's Trumpet Voluntary while Gilbert donned a bow tie and theatrically pronounced:

"My dear Esme, it's been far too long since I've seen your cloaca. Do please let me have a little look." As the boys pinned Sanderson down, Connors prodded the violin bow into Sanderson's crotch.

"Oh, Iain, I thought you'd forgotten all about my cloaca," wailed Sanderson. "It may be a bit rusty, but a bit of oil could do the trick, like it did with your car last year."

"An excellent idea, my dear. Lubrication is a wonderful thing to get the old cogs going, but I fear this may be a WD40 job. I'll get some from the garage." Creased with laughter, Hemsworth reminded the others that the cross-country run was due to start in ten minutes.

On account of his asthma, Edward was exempted from the run, so instead went for a walk, his task being to find three different stages of nature. He collected closed and opened pine cones, dandelions in flower and gone to seed, a caterpillar and, very fortunately, a chrysalis found nestling behind some rotten bark, both of which he housed in a discarded cigarette packet. He felt happy with his finds and his own company and would have liked to drop in at Elm Cottage for an ice cream, but Mr Saunders was on marshal duty at the finish line.

Mr Catchpole greeted the boys enthusiastically at the next Club meeting.

"Good Evening, Grovers, I can see that you have taken up the challenge with great aplomb, and Mrs Catchpole and myself will guess your identities. If in doubt, we are permitted three questions and those that are asked the most questions will be awarded a prize. Now, line up, and Mrs Catchpole and myself will attempt to catch you out.

Connors was instantly recognisable, sporting a blond wig, a pale blue frock with a starched white apron, white ankle socks and black pumps.

"Alice in Wonderland, Connors, and with no mistaking. But you are missing the Alice band. Did any of you know where the phrase comes from? You see, there is always learning to be done whilst having fun. Now, Hemsworth, your character looks intriguing and, if I may say so, you haven't put in too much effort to impersonate a girl. Is that because you find it embarrassing?"

"No, Sir, not at all. I just thought I'd keep you all guessing."

"Quite right, dear boy."

Clad in baggy, dark blue shorts and a tatty brown short-sleeved shirt, torn at the pocket and a pair of gym shoes, his shins were muddy and he was carrying a dog lead.

"This is very intriguing, is it not, my dear. Would you like to get a clue from the ruffian?"

The softly spoken Mrs Catchpole, barely audible, enquired, "Do you have a girl's name?"

"No, I don't, Ma'am," replied Hemsworth.

Mrs Catchpole continued, "Well, you are obviously a tom-boy and there are not many of those in great children's literature."

"Sir, my clue is that I don't believe you would consider the creator of my character to have written great children's literature, only profuse children's literature."

"Ah hah! There we have it," exclaimed Mr Catchpole. "Might you be missing a dog called Timmy?" Hemsworth beamed and the boys applauded. "Although," he added, "I do hope you are not still reading The Famous Five, dear boy, as you will never get in to Marlborough if you are!"

Gilbert was also simply clad in a long, coarse, grey, empire-line dress of harsh fabric, wearing a wig of a tight bun and sensible lace-up shoes. Mr Catchpole considered.

"You look poor and plain. Are you in service?"

"Yes I am, Sir, and my character is not strictly from children's literature."

Mrs Catchpole, blushing slightly, proffered, "And did you fall in love with your employer?"

"Yes I did, Ma'am."

"A pertinent question, my dear, and I think we can be in no doubt that our heroine is Jane Eyre."

Sanderson's guise was a black-belted, frilly red-checked, knee-length dress with red patent high heels and a short, dark curly wig.

"You make a fine Dorothy, Sanderson. Well done. It was the shoes that gave you away. Our last but not least, contestant is Taylor in a nun's habit and his prop is a guitar."

Chosen deliberately as he still had an unbroken treble voice, Taylor then gave a rendition of 'The hills are alive...' and evening was brought to a close. Hemsworth and Gilbert were awarded a small box of Quality Street to share on account of being asked two questions each.

"Grovers, I wish you an enjoyable half term, and please give some thought to the hobbies you would like to be known for in Debrett's Peerage and why, in preparation for our next Cloaca Club meeting in three weeks time."

The following Friday, Mr Saunders carried Edward's small, initialled leather suitcase up to the spare room of the cottage. It was to be his last stay there because his parents were taking him to see Der Rosenkavalier at Glyndebourne on the last exeat of term. The weather was cool, overcast and not promising for the outdoor activities Mr Saunders had planned. During last year's summer half term he had taught Edward to cast and fly fish on the chalk stream which meandered along the valley, separating the school's boundary from the neighbouring estate. His plans for their first supper, being to barbeque sausages and bake potatoes on an open fire in the garden, were abandoned because of the fine rain, and he was instead preparing supper in the kitchen whilst Edward was absorbed in a copy of *Decline and Fall* in the sitting room. His reading age was much higher than his actual one, and he devoured Evelyn Waugh, Trollope and Dickens.

It must have been the cooking of sausages, beans and mash, Adrian's favourite, which had brought a memory back. Adrian Buckmaster, whose parents were missionaries in Africa, had been Edward's predecessor. As a prefect, Adrian had been a member of The Cloaca Club and had divulged his secret during a summer picnic a-deux, having drunk a pint of cider. Mr Saunders had had no idea of the existence of the Club and was agog. He had unwisely passed on the information to Edward several years later, when smoking his first catch of a brown trout on the riverbank in his portable smoker. Mr Saunders felt an urge to revisit the topic, but squashed it. Instead, after supper, they played racing demon and made plans to go to the cinema in Newbury the following day.

The first Star Wars film had just been released and was already a mega box-office hit, but neither of them particularly enjoyed it, not being fans of unlikely characters and loud noise. Driving back to the cottage Edward was quiet, and, in tune with his feelings, Mr Saunders chose his moment. He placed his left hand on Edward's inner thigh, moving it up slowly to feel that soft, sacred and secret place. This was to be just the prelude for their last evening at Elm Cottage. Edward didn't react.

"I'm going to miss your stays here, Edward, but I will come and see you. Are you looking forward to starting at Eton?"

"Yes and no, Sir. I shall miss you too. You've been very kind to me."

"Edward, I shouldn't be telling you this, but you particularly excelled in your Common Entrance English papers, scoring the highest mark in the country. We're all very proud of you obtaining a scholarship. The school has never produced a King's scholar to Eton before."

"I have you to thank for that, Sir. The title I chose for my essay was 'A Club I would like to belong to', so I wrote about Cloaca."

Mr Saunders drew in his breath, slightly swerving the car, as his future and the future of Diseased Park flashed before him.

THE TUNER 1987

for Sam and Alan

Becky let herself into the flat. She had come straight home from school as it was her birthday and she so hoped that what she'd asked for would be waiting for her. The flat seemed oddly quiet without Classic FM playing in the background or her mother playing the piano.

"Mum?"

Silence. The horrific carnage that met her eyes was unbelievable, starting at the end of the hall with a large pool of blood and her mother lying half-naked on her side by the fireplace, surrounded by a sea of debris of sawdust, feathers, millet, blood and broken ornaments. Beside her was an upturned birdcage, its poor yellow inhabitant frantically flapping about. Becky screamed, vomited into a large pot plant and rang 999. Whilst waiting for the police and ambulance to arrive, she checked her mother's diary to see what the entries were for the day but she didn't touch anything, neither the birdcage nor its distressed occupant. That was hard as it was the present she had so wished for.

That morning in northeast London, Matt found Jason Bridge struggling with his entry fob key while bearing sack-like, tightly packed bags under each arm. "Groats," Jason announced as Matt held the front door open for him.

"Beg your pardon?" Matt replied, stepping back feigning comical alarm.

"For the budgies."

"Of course."

As usual, no eye contact was made during this exchange. Jason Bridge avoided eye contact and if possible conversation. He was definitely an odd fellow – lanky, pale-skinned, with sharp features and sunken eyes. His thin, black hair flopped greasily around his tortoiseshell-rimmed spectacles. Matt had never seen him in anything other than a dark blue tracksuit and worn, high-backed dirty trainers on his large feet.

Matt found himself thinking about Jason Bridge and his habits as he drove out to Epping for an unwelcomingly early tuning at half-past nine. It had annoyed him that Jason's unwieldy van was half-parked across his own space, and not for the first time. In the passenger foot well of his car were cassettes ranging from Frank Sinatra to Meatloaf. Having perfect pitch he couldn't bear to listen to Classic FM or Radio 3 – or even to go to concerts – as an out of tune F sharp in one of the instruments caused him severe offence. Mrs Carter wasn't one of his special clients so he was able to charge her full rates and she was reasonably local. Her second-hand, but new to her, piano had been delivered a month ago so would have now settled for tuning. She was watering pot plants outside her front door as Matt arrived, and a large ginger cat lolled beside her on the warm paving stones.

"Good morning, Mr Moss. Do come in. I'm so pleased with the new piano. Here she is."

Matt and the cat followed Mrs Carter inside. One look at the shiny black Japanese upright Atlas told Matt immediately that this was not the piano he had checked out for her at the music shop in Ongar prior to purchase. He lifted the top off, shone his torch in to verify his suspicions and sat down to play. He always remembered every piano's action. When Mrs Carter appeared with a tray of coffee and shortbread biscuits, Matt broke the news. "Mrs Carter, I'm afraid this is not the piano I looked at for you. It has two pedals, not three, and the serial number is different. I made a note of the original one." He produced a small leather notebook and showed Mrs Carter the entry. She went into a complete spin. "Oh, Mr Moss, how clever of you, but what are we going to do now? This is a despicable trick and they have such a good reputation too. Maybe it was a mistake with the delivery."

Matt doubted it as she had been short-changed about a thousand pounds worth of piano. "Leave it to me, Mrs Carter, and I'll ring them now if I may use your phone," thus saving his own mobile credit. Despite his life being rather haphazard and chaotic, Matt was good in a crisis and had a calm, reassuring manner and the situation was resolved. The wrong piano to be exchanged for the correct one in a few days' time, the original showroom one still being available, as he knew it would be.

Aside from his bread-and-butter clients, whom he tended to tune for in the evenings after they returned from work, he took on a totally different attitude with his younger, more attractive lady ones: smiley, slightly bumbling and gauche, and all the while assessing them for their possibility as bed partners. After first tuning, he would play his well-worn reportoire of Mozart and Bach, and then improvised jazz before making a sudden departure. He found this a technique that worked well as most of these clients were ladies of leisure, having taken up the piano again while their husbands worked long hours or travelled and while their children were at school.

Of course his success rate wasn't a hundred per cent, more like sixty to seventy, but as he left it up to his clients to make the first move he wasn't in danger of losing business. Good at reading their signs and body language, Matt was a safe and easy lover, completely outside their social circles and totally beyond suspicion from their hard-working and ignorant husbands. He usually got free sex once a week and when tunings were cancelled and not re-booked, the arrangement ended without fuss or demand.

Matt kept his charges competitively low for all his special lady clients to ensure their regular six-monthly tunings would be booked in advance, rather like a dental appointment. He charged more for his male customers and top whack for the occasional tunings he did at The Wigmore Hall before concerts and during the interval. He could earn a hundred pounds for public tunings, but they tended to be in the evenings when he was usually two sheets to the wind and his tuning not as sharp as it should have been. His only hope that the audience wouldn't notice after a few glasses themselves at the Hall bar.

In between geographically arranged tunings, Matt usually found a pub or bar to down a few double vodka and tonics or a couple of large glasses of house white wine. He resented paying over-inflated prices for poor pub grub, the hostelries he preferred not being the newly-popular gastro pubs. Instead, he enjoyed drinking by himself and felt more comfortable not being surrounded by dining couples or ladies who lunched in cosy, worn surroundings. Usually, he would not bother to eat until he got home in the late afternoon and more often than not, finished off the evening at his local, within walking distance, to down several pints and sometimes playing the honky-tonk piano for more free ones.

Jason Bridge lived below Matt in the ground floor flat of a low-rise council block. He had a pretty endless stream of male visitors, some clutching small cages, some not and – most regularly – a strapping and handsome man of about thirty. Matt occasionally bumped into Jason at the local launderette, where he had learned extensively about the habits of budgerigars, which was, as Jason had told him, "A male hobby". Matt found the subject oddly interesting, which was just as well because Jason had no other topics of conversation.

There was absolutely nothing that Jason did not know about budgies: Spangles, Pieds, Lutinos, Albinos and Sky Blues. His interest was instilled at an early age by his maternal grandmother, with whom he'd lived after his mother died when he was thirteen. She had bought him a Lutino budgie, yellow in colour, and he was besotted by Layla, as he had named her, after the famous pop song.

Lutinos were less common than other breeds of budgies and on account of their colour were often mistaken for canaries to the casual eye. Jason had heard a programme on Radio 4 about animal hoarding, which was classified as owning more than thirty of the same species. At any one time he had between forty and fifty budgies housed in his large, heated garden shed, but they were quiet and kept meticulously clean so he was under no threat of having them taken away by the authorities. Unlike barking dogs or urinating cats, they didn't bother the neighbours. He showed his prize birds all over the country during the July to November seaon, the calendar highlight being the annual World Budgerigar Show in Doncaster. There, up to 4,000 birds were exhibited, being kept quiet under the fitted covers on their cages to prevent distress until they were proudly taken into the arena for judging in their varied catagories. Four first prize-winners could net him £200, but he had yet to achieve a Best in Show. The income they generated was from private purchasers by word of mouth.

Like any animal owner, Jason had his favourite birds, not necessarily the show ones, and when they died at between six and eight years, he mourned and missed them. At huge expense and totally beyond his means, he had had eight of his most treasured ones stuffed and mounted by a taxidermist in Islington. This macabre procedure involved delivering their frozen corpses wrapped in polythene in a shoe box with their date of death written on top. They flanked the framed certificate for being a fully registered member of The Budgerigar Society on a shelf in his sitting room, and their beady, unblinking eyes stared down at him accusingly from their glass cases.

The day after seeing Mrs Carter, Matt had a first-time tuning appointment at a block of mansion flats in Chiswick during the late morning. This was further than he usually travelled, but he had been highly recommended and as it was not a part of London with which he was familiar, he could find a new pub, which he always looked forward to. He twice pressed the buzzer named Hamilton-Morris and was puzzled that there was no reply. So he found a shabby bar in Chiswick High Road and downed a couple of vodkas (not detectable on his breath) whilst completing the Guardian crossword. After an hour or so he returned to the mansion block, but still no answer. Next he rang Mrs Hamilton-Morris. The call went onto answerphone, and as it was such a hot and humid day, he decided to drive back home to watch Wimbledon. He could have sworn that he saw Jason's distinctive dark green van parked down a side street in Hammersmith.

Back home, Matt went into his bedroom to change into a pair of shorts and noticed Jason coming inside from his shed with a cage. Wimbledon was in full swing and he made himself a strong cup of tea and rolled a large joint from a soft ball of pungent dope tightly in foil, stored in a plastic camera film canister behind some books. Ladies Singles were on, and a new player who he hadn't seen before grunted loudly while playing her shots and he found himself waiting for the grunts rather than focusing on the match. The stuff was much stronger than usual, having been obtained from the Rastafarian who sometimes worked on his car from a greasy garage in a nearby railway arch, and it wasn't long before Matt wasn't sure whether he was watching a game of grunts or a game of tennis. He became convinced that the players seemed to be coming out of his television screen and grunting at him, so he turned it off. The regular and loudening grunts had had the effect of arousing him and he exfoliated himself, in a manner of speaking, having forgotten that he had just eaten half a tub of Pringles.

On his way to the corner shop that afternoon, Jason took his black bags out to the bin area at the side of the flats for collection the next morning. He always produced a lot of rubbish, mostly generated by the budgies' damp newspaper and wood shavings. He walked to the local shop to buy digestive biscuits, milk, marmalade and six ready-meal frozen shepherd's pies, which were a weekly bulk-buy.

Matt awoke several hours later, thirsty and starving hungry. He ordered a take-away curry and (not wishing to drive) six large cans of Special Brew and a bottle of vodka from a local alcohol-delivery service, Bella Bottle, who delivered within half an hour and took cash or card. This was rather an extravagant way of buying booze and at nearly double supermarket prices, but the one thing he could not risk losing was his driving licence.

After a couple of cans and consuming an obscene amount of over-ordered curry he rolled himself another joint and settled down to watch the nine o'clock news. Just thirty-six days before her untimely death, Christies had auctioned a lot of Princess Diana's clothes for $5.5m, and Space Shuttle M-34 had collided with and damaged the Mir Space Station, while in the USA, the Supreme Court upheld the doctor-assisted suicide ban. The dope taking its fanciful effect again, he decided he would like to go into space and would look into what becoming an astronaut entailed in the morning.

Some time later, whilst half watching a film, he became aware of blue flashing lights outside the front of the flats. Paranoid that the police had come to confiscate his drugs with no sirens so as not to alert him, he hurriedly flushed the plastic canister and butt ends from the ashtray down his toilet. The canister floated, so he removed it and put it at the bottom of his pedal bin. A discreet peep through the window revealed Jason's handsome friend dressed up as a policeman, talking into his radio device on the small lawn, and then the shouting started. When he saw Jason, handcuffed by two policemen, being escorted into one of the police cars he became convinced that what he was experiencing was an elaborate episode of paranoia or a weird dream. It was only when his doorbell buzzed that reality kicked in. He briefly considered spraying some air freshener about the place, but decided it would be suspicious, so he hurriedly lit a normal cigarette. He tried to behave normally as he went with trepidation to open the door, figuring that if Jason had been arrested they wouldn't raid him. Unwisely, but out of nerves, he greeted the policeman jovially with "Aye aye, Sir," which he immediately regretted as it was ridiculously light-hearted and inappropriate.

After extensive questioning at the police station and subsequently being released, Matt strolled home in the early hours as the dawn was breaking. He could look forward to a special tuning booked for 11.30 that morning, while the budgies, up and chirruping their dawn chorus, waited for their breakfast. They would wait all day before the RSPB came to re-home them.

FLOWERS FOR ALBA 2017

for Alba

Alba didn't know she was being stalked.

On Friday nights it was her habit to buy flowers for the weekend from a stall outside Belsize Park tube station, having told her husband that only men guilty of an affair or a secret brought their wives flowers – unless it was for their birthday or a special occasion.

That Friday Alba was, as always, greeted warmly by Sergio. "My Bella, you're late this evening. What would my Bella like? The lilies were so beautiful today, but they all sold quickly and I have no white flowers left other than the alstroemerias." Alba only ever bought white flowers in season: anenomes, hyacinths, gerberas, tulips, freesias, lily of the valley, canna lilies, hydrangeas, peonies, orchids. She settled for the alstroemerias and produced a ten-pound note from her wallet. "But, my Bella, this is not a good choice as they last for so long and maybe you won't come again next Friday? And no, you cannot pay for them because alstroemerias always have to be given. It is an ancient tradition - they symbolise friendship and devotion. Please, a gift for my Bella from Sergio. I think of you as my Bella, but what is your name? Please?"

She smiled demurely. "I'll give you a clue, Sergio: my name means the colour of the flowers I buy from you."

"Your name is white – or maybe Bianca?"

"Not exactly. It's Alba, which means white. It's a Latin name."

"How wonderfully romantic. I've never heard that name before."

Alba took the expected, idle flattery in her stride and, with the blooms duly wrapped and accepted, she made the short walk home. As she always carried a briefcase, was well dressed and had an air of authority, Sergio imagined that she might be a surgeon or a doctor, or maybe a professor. He had conjectured her name would be romantic or poetic, maybe Clementine or Juliet or Lynette, as immortalised by Tennyson's epic poem.

After his English public school education, Sergio had briefly attended Cambridge to study English literature before being sent down for being a nuisance to the college Bursar's wife. Whilst waiting to inherit his father's money and (lesser Italian nobility) title of Conte da Verdici, he indulged his passion for flowers and had purchased the old-fashioned wooden stall from an old boy who had owned it and the pitch for some forty years.

About three months previously and on several other occasions, Sergio had followed Alba home to her house in Primrose Gardens. He'd watched her let herself in the front door and draw the curtains before returning to his unattended stall. There was no point in hanging around there during the day as most mornings he saw her going into the tube station just before half-past eight; sometimes she gave him a little wave.

The following Friday, having over-stocked with white flowers from Covent Garden early that morning, Sergio waited until ten o'clock at night, but Alba didn't come. His hopes were dashed again the following week, when her much-awaited visit again did not materialise. So Sergio made a plan.

Early the next morning he wheeled his flower stall to outside 16 Primrose Gardens with a banner draped over the top saying "Flowers for Alba". The road obstruction's ensuing commotion caused Alba's husband to get up, draw the curtains and look outside.

"My God," he exclaimed. "What's all this about, Alba? I think you have some explaining to do!"

FANTASMA 2006

for Caroline

The ticket machine at Termini was unduly complicated and, with her limited Italian, Geraldine hoped she had validated her ticket correctly and wouldn't be prosecuted on the train. Leaving the dull, low-rise blocks outside Rome, with their graffiti and gaudy hoardings, advertising unfamiliar films and faces, the scenery gave way to parched allotments and uncultivated countryside. White plastic chairs surrounded makeshift shelters with corrugated roofs in the mud-cracked fields, where ancient tractors and tethered donkeys, their heads lowered in the relentless midday heat, flashed past between the tunnels. Derelict dwellings, pylons and scrub were not the scenery Geraldine had anticipated on the forty-five minute journey north to Orvieto. Where were the green wine terraces, lakes, umbrella pines and soft undulating hills her mother had so often spoken about? She began to question her choice of destination and wondered whether she should have gone to Tuscany instead.

Having recently lost her mother, Geraldine was going to

a small, family-run hotel near Orvieto with the intention of writing, or starting to write, a novel. The two weeks were much looked forward to, but also dreaded for fear of failure. A few members of the writing group she belonged to had recommended going away to a quiet Italian hotel, with few facilities and no children; and amongst her mother's large amount of paperwork Geraldine had found a battered card of The Hotel Villa di Raphaello, but they had never been there together. This was particularly odd because her mother had come from Orvieto.

Having spent twenty years running a small maps and prints gallery in Fitzrovia, inherited from her uncle, she had returned to Lincolnshire to look after her mother in her final months. In her late forties and unmarried, she was an avid member of local clubs in her home town of Stamford: reading, writing, psychic studies and an art group. She felt at home amongst the attractive Georgian architecture and cobbled streets, and through the cultural aspect of the town had quickly made like-minded friends, two of whom had recommended Umbria.

When the taxi turned into the short drive bordered with Cypresses, her spirits lifted. The 16th century medium-sized villa was exactly as promised: stone, with large patches of flaking rendering, tall turquoise shutters and a terracotta pantile roof. Certificates and awards covered the top pane of the glass front door, which led into a large hall with red and cream octagonal floor tiles. A central chandelier hung from the high-beamed ceiling, and heavy oak furniture and chintz armchairs formed the reception and waiting area.

A stony-faced lady of indeterminate age sat at the wooden reception, fiddling with her hair.

"Buon Giorno," she grunted.

"Buon Giorno, Signora. Geraldine Wyatt. I've booked for two weeks."

"Suo passaporto, per favore."

Geraldine submitted her passport. The signora shuffled some paperwork under the counter and took one of the keys off the row of brass hooks, gesturing Geraldine to follow as she plodded up the staircase, her sizeable rear resembling a manatee.

"Signora, scusi: my luggage?" Geraldine pointed to her suitcases.

"Si, Francesco. Francesco, bagaglio camera quattro," she bellowed.

At the top of the wide, brass-rodded staircase was a spacious landing, with a faded red carpet and doors leading off. With no grace whatsoever, the signora unlocked her bedroom and pointed out the bathroom, safe and mini-bar. She had obviously been given a room at the back of the hotel as the window was high up and small, with no view. Geraldine felt disappointed, claustrophobic and unwelcome, and stood for a while to consider her choices. The bedrooms on the hotel's website all had small balconies and appeared light and airy.

Returning her key to reception a few minutes later, the charmer did not look up from her newspaper, so Geraldine hit the small brass bell with force.

"Signora, mia camera. Mia camera is dark and I would like to have a room with a balcony, per favore."

The old bat only had a limited rat-run of English, with no intention of increasing her vocabulary, but Geraldine's tone and the returning of the key had been understood. After tutting and rising reluctantly, the signora decided that the guest was obviously going to be difficult, so she would put her in Room 12. That would serve her right.

Room 12 was beautiful: light and fresh, painted powder blue, with tall French doors leading onto a small iron fretwork balcony overlooking the swimming pool. Geraldine thought she had finally arrived and forgave the grumpy old so-and-so for trying to palm her off with a sub-standard room.

Having unpacked, and after the long, hot journey, the swimming pool beckoned. There was just one late middle-aged couple on the sunbeds, both reading Harry Potter. Geraldine wished them a good afternoon.

"Good afternoon, have you just arrived?" the man with a hefty paunch enquired in a northern accent.

"Yes, this afternoon. Isn't it lovely here. I'm Geraldine. How do you do."

"Welcome, Geraldine, I'm David, and this is my wife, Kay. We've been coming here for six years running now, and it never changes, does it, love? Nor do the staff. They just get older and a little more crotchety each year – especially Elvira." Geraldine was pleased they had already found something in common and also relieved that she would have people to talk to, if needed.

Two sides of the pool were surrounded by quivering poplars, laurel, hydrangeas, acacias, mimosa, and a few wilting white rose bushes. The sound of digging machinery was not far away and David explained there was quarrying going on nearby. Other than that, the birds were singing, and the chorus of cicadas sounded like crickets on cocaine. After a couple of hours soaking up the sun, surroundings and the sweet smell of eucalyptus, Geraldine felt relaxed and at home. David and Kay informed her that there was no restaurant at the hotel as such, but Elvira or Francesco could provide light meals on the terrace. "There are some lovely restaurants in Orvieto, mind you," David continued, "and we've hired a car. You're most welcome to join us for supper tonight."

"That is very kind, but I think I'll eat in quietly this evening. See you tomorrow."

"Arrivederci, Geraldine. See you domani and have a nice evening."

When she was out of earshot, Kay said, "Oh, that's a shame, isn't it love? She seems rather an interesting character. Maybe she'll join us tomorrow."

After a lengthy bath, Geraldine inspected the mini-bar and opened a half bottle of chilled, unfamiliar white wine, which had a garlicky taste and was rather unpleasant. Disappointingly, there was no writing desk in her bedroom, but she would write on the terrace; it was shaded and heavily canopied by tumbling wisteria and visiting bees, accommodating several small white wrought-iron tables and chairs. Supper was simple: a selection of salami, prosciutto and bresaola, with some mature Italian cheese and chunks of slightly stale, white, crusty bread, accompanied by a saucer of pungent, dark olive oil and a bowl of fruit. It was delicious.

Elvira had been replaced at reception by Francesco, an elderly, kindly-looking gentleman with a whiskery moustache and a gentle, round face. He gestured where the dining room was.

"Signora, domani. Breakfast from eight to ten. Buona notte, signora."

Geraldine placed the black and white photograph of her mother, which must have been taken when she was in her early twenties, on her bedside table. She was a classic Italian beauty – poised, with a dreamy look and large, watery eyes. She had married a young English officer billeted in Italy at the end of the war, but had seldom talked about her childhood, claiming memory loss. There was once some reference to losing her twin sister tragically, which was never spoken of again. In fact there was a lot that she didn't know about her mother. She had been distant, and suffered from nerves and anxiety. Geraldine's childhood had been a lonely one, and she had entertained herself with books, painting and imaginary friends, whilst her mother played endless games of Patience.

Too tired to read, Geraldine quickly fell asleep and had vivid, unfathomable dreams of her mother being chased by stampeding wild pigs. She often had dreams where she was attempting to protect her mother. Nevertheless, she awoke refreshed, and the opened shutters promised a hot and still day with not a cloud in the sky.

Breakfast was the usual continental fare. A plump, blonde lady, clad in orange shorts and a yellow monogrammed T-shirt, was helping herself to copious quantities of the rather uninviting cooked option.

"Guten Morgen," she beamed, whilst being joined by a thin teenage girl with a sullen expression.

"Good morning."

As the dining room was dark, oppressive and smelled vaguely of disinfectant, Geraldine took her breakfast out to the terrace. Tall, whispering bamboo and eucalpytus trees sloped down a steep bank to a dried-up river bed, and large terracotta planters with wilting contents separated the terrace from the lawn adjoining the drive.

Well aware that the first sentence of a book should be captivating, she had deliberately left this critical moment until now. Papers spread out and pen poised, this is what she had come to do, and it was just as daunting as anticipated. By way of salvation, David and Kay appeared and ordered cappuccinos. They greeted Geraldine warmly.

"Buon giorno, Geraldine. How was your night?"

"I slept well, thank you. Good morning."

"We've just been to visit the cathedral before it gets too hot," David enthused, drawing up a couple of chairs to her table. "May we join you?"

"Please, of course."

"It's one of the finest cathedrals in Italy," he continued, "the elaborate carvings of beasts and animals on the outside are incredible and the mosaics amazing. We visit it every year and always find something new, don't we, love?"

"This time," chimed in Kay with a naughty smile, "it was strange monkeys with, well, you know. You'll have to go and see for yourself."

"Yes, I will. My mother was married in Orvieto cathedral," came the unexpected reply.

"No way!" Kay exclaimed. "You kept that a bit quiet. How incredible. You must tell us more. Maybe over dinner in town this evening?"

"Thank you, but I really must get on with my work, and if I make good progress today I expect I'll be tired tonight. Maybe tomorrow."

"What are you up to there, Geraldine?" enquired David. "I hope you haven't brought work to do on holiday?"

"No, not at all. I am a writer," came the confident reply.

"A writer. How interesting. We don't know any authors, do we, love? We're just humble northerners and run a nursing home in Cleethorpes. It does us well though, doesn't it, love. We have good staff and they keep things ticking over when we go away. We go on holiday a fair bit and never need worry."

"Oh, that's good." Geraldine had no experience of nursing homes and wasn't sure how to conclude the conversation. They were chatterboxes and showed no signs of leaving her alone.

"We like the lakes too, don't we, David. Especially Como in the autumn."

"Mind you," David continued, "we're not averse to Provence either, are we, love?" He rose and clapped his hands together. "Well, we should leave the author to write in peace, shouldn't we, love. See you later, Geraldine, and don't forget that offer of dinner with us."

"She's a dark horse, isn't she," said Kay conspiratorially as they went upstairs.

"And I get the feeling that there will always be some excuse not to come out with us."

Geraldine decided to explore the grounds of the hotel, which were not extensive. A wiry, bow-legged old man with a lined, leathery face was skulking about with a twig broom, half-heartedly sweeping up small, crispy leaves from the lawns and paths. The German lady and her daughter were sunbathing by the pool with headphones on, throbbing annoyingly, reading magazines. The water looked tempting, so Geraldine changed, fetched her book and took the sunbed furthest away, but it was too hot to read and she drifted off for over an hour, waking during the early afternoon. After swimming a few lengths, she started her reading club book for that month, but her thoughts kept turning guiltily to the reason for the trip and her writing club's suggestion of a target of a thousand words a day. She didn't want to disappoint her enthusiastic yet competitive friends, nor indeed herself, but getting started was proving just as difficult as she had feared. Deciding to give lunch a miss, she had a shower and took a taxi into Orvieto for an early supper and a change of scene.

Her taxi meandered up the steep hill to the town and left her in the main Square, promising to return in two hours. The narrow streets were crammed with buzzing restaurants, bars, cafes, gelaterias, cheap clothes, underwear shops and a few exotic fooderies. She purchased three bottles of Orvieto white from a small, random, supermarket, which also curiously sold Maldon salt. And also two bottles of local vino rosso, not trusting the quality of the choice from the mini-bar, before choosing a more upmarket, quieter restaurant on the edge of the Square. She ordered osso bucco and a half bottle of house red. The view from the restaurant's *terrazza* overlooked the verdant, terraced valley and was very beautiful, but she was conscious of not making the most of the experience. There was something unsettling about the atmosphere in the hotel, which she believed was hindering her writing. As she ordered a selection of gelati and a glass of dessert wine a bohemian-looking couple came up to her table. He had a long ponytail and the woman had purple hair and was dripping in silver bangles and necklaces.

"Summertons Maps and Prints?" enquired the man, giving Geraldine a start.

"It's Damien and Lois. We lived in the first floor flat opposite your husband's Gallery in Russell Street all those years ago. Remember us? But we didn't stay there long after your husband died and you took over, so maybe you don't."

"He wasn't my husband actually. He was my uncle." Geraldine blushed.

"Your uncle? We thought you were a couple, although obviously he was much older than you. But several young women came and went over the years."

"No, I'm sorry, I don't remember you, and I'm finding this conversation quite intrusive. Please leave me alone." The couple shrugged and left her to eat her pudding in peace.

Geraldine tried to gather her thoughts as she entered the cathedral. It was not the moment to remember Oliver, nor that whole episode in her life, which had been a huge and heart-breaking mistake. She tried to absorb the cool and calm of the cathedral and to imagine her mother walking up the long, marbled aisle through the rood screen to the high altar, before kneeling to make her marriage vows. It was almost as if her mother had sent those dreadful people to remind and punish her. She wasn't in the right frame of mind to appreciate the beauty and architecture of the surroundings, and went back to the steps where her taxi had dropped her off.

Sleep eluded Geraldine that night, and her thoughts kept returning to her mother. The relationship with her parents had been severed for several years when she lived with Oliver, her father's younger brother (and that was at their suggestion), while she studied textiles at Central St. Martins after leaving school. The whole business was unfortunate, but she had at least inherited the gallery, which had given her both employment and financial independence.

Her dreams that night were again dark and vivid. She was surrounded by crashing waterfalls and deep, muddy, pale green pools, smelling of sulphur. People everywhere were smearing themselves with mud and shouting joyfully, while the hot springs cascaded over them. There was nowhere to put her bag, and then she couldn't find it. Awaking with a jolt, her room felt cold and a lady was standing at the foot of her bed. Geraldine turned on the bedside lamp and the lady was gone. The nightmares were just as bad as at home, but there was no way that her medication could be reduced for fear of another period of heavy depression. She was reconciled to the side effects of a high dosage of drugs to combat her bipolar disorder, and the nocturnal hallucinations were of small consequence compared with existing in an endlessly dark abyss. For most of her adult life she had been prescribed many different anti-depressants, none of which helped, and she couldn't tolerate lithium. It was only after a two-month episode of extreme mania, high activity and not sleeping that bipolar 2 was correctly diagnosed. The pills almost instantly corrected and balanced her, and she had been able to function and live normally ever since. On reflection, her mother must have suffered with the same affliction, but was never diagnosed.

Drained by the nightmares, she was in no mood to start writing the following day, which passed quickly and was free of unwanted interruptions. She started reading her book again, but it wasn't that good. Her writing club had told her to 'Read, read, read'. This was a tall order when you were attempting to find the time to start writing yourself. That evening, having only eaten a Kit-Kat and a packet of salted almonds from the mini-bar for supper, Geraldine took a bath and an early night, but again sleep didn't come easily. Despite the heat of the evening – apparently the temperature was ten degrees hotter than normal for July – her bedroom felt chilly. Knowing the soporific effect of her medication and more alcohol than usual, she poured herself a glass of red wine and sipped it on the balcony. And another one, before falling into a deep slumber.

The lady was there again when she awoke shortly after midnight. She looked familiar, and Geraldine swore she was not dreaming. Strangely, she wasn't frightened, as her psychic studies had given her an interest in the occult. She would make her enquiries in the morning.

Elvira was on duty at reception, picking at her fingernails, in front of an ancient, bulky computer screen. She didn't stir, but Geraldine had come prepared and had looked up the Italian translation for ghost in her small Collins dictionary.

"Buon giorno, signora."

Elvira turned and raised her eyes, still wearing the same grim expression.

"Buon giorno," she replied, her lips hardly moving.

"Signora," Geraldine continued, "mia camera – una fantasma? A signora?"

Elvira frowned and shook her head.

"But, Signora, there is a signora in my bedroom and I've seen her twice."

"No."

"No? Do you understand what I am saying, Signora?"

The conversation seemingly concluded, Geraldine ordered a cappucino and went out to the terrace. It was not the outcome she had hoped for.

A new young Italian couple were having breakfast and David and Kay were studying a map.

"Buon giorno, Geraldine. We didn't see you yesterday. Are you enjoying your stay and getting on well with your writing?"

"Yes, thank you. It's a very inspiring place to write."

David continued: "We're going out for the day to visit Saturnia as we have never been before, have we, love? It is quite a long drive and on B roads, about two hours."

"Saturnia?" asked Geraldine.

"Yes. Hot volcanic sulphurous springs apparently in the middle of fields, where wild boar roam. The natural springs are 37 degrees in temperature and the mud has healing properties. Kay has a bit of arthritis in her knees, so we are hoping for a natural cure, aren't we, love? Oh, and have you heard about the train bombings in Mumbai? Another terrorist attack and over 700 people injured."

"No, how awful," Geraldine responded, "but I hope you have a lovely day."

She felt a cold shiver flood through her.

With the information David had imparted, there was no way she felt like putting pen to paper. Her head was spinning and not in the right space to take on starting her novel. She didn't know what to do next, so went down to the pool to think and sunbathe. Having skipped breakfast, she needed to eat at midday and ordered a plate of tricolore from Elvira. Preparing the lunch herself, Elvira spat onto the sliced beef tomatoes and turned them over before adding mozzarella, rocket and a sprig of basil to the platter, delivering it to Geraldine with a basket of bread. So fresh and so tasty, Geraldine thought. Somehow these ingredients never tasted so good at home.

After lunch she went up to her room and lay on the bed. She missed the familiarity of Stamford and her structured day-to-day routine. She felt confused, unsettled but, most of all, guilty for not starting to write.

Deciding to have her evening drink and supper on the terrace, Francesco was on duty at reception. She ordered a glass of red wine, but had no appetite. The Italian couple were enjoying a bottle of prosecco and chatting away happily. The house red was surprisingly drinkable and Geraldine went to order another glass as a ruse to speak to Francesco.

"Signor, per favore: mia camera – una fantasma, a signora." Francesco coughed and nodded.

"Si, signora. Viviana. You see Viviana." Was that it? Again the language barrier prevented further explanations, so she returned to the terrace and approached the young Italian couple.

"Scusi, per favore. You speak English?"

"Yes, but not so much," the young woman replied.

"Thank you. Please can you help me?"

Geraldine explained what she needed and the couple followed

her back to reception, where a long and heated dialogue ensued with Francesco.

"Ecco," the girl finally said. "The lady you see is the sister of Francesco and Elvira. Before the Montanari family make the villa into hotel, she die in 1950..."

"Stop. Stop there. Did you say Montanari? That was my mother's maiden name."

This information was passed on to Francesco, who looked quizzical.

"Your room was her bedroom," the girl continued. "The lady, Viviana, had, how you say, 'epilessia'." The young woman jerked about before continuing.

"She drown when she is twenty five, when Elvira is only twelve years."

"Drowned?"

Another exchange took place with Francesco, and Geraldine picked up the word 'Saturnia'.

"She drown when visiting Saturnia with Elvira and Francesco," the girl continued. "Is very sad for the family, and her twin sister had already leave Italy to go to England. Viviana only visit your bedroom."

Francesco produced an A4 black and white photograph from a metal filing cabinet and wiped the dust off. Viviana was a dead-ringer for Geraldine's mother, and on the reverse of the photograph was the same circular stamp of 'The Oscar Studios, London, W.1', with 1948 pencilled underneath. Viviana had been her aunt, and this explained a lot about her mother.

Geraldine cut short her visit by ten days. It was time to leave. On the train she felt elated and inspired by her short stay at the hotel. She hadn't experienced that level of emotional charge since falling in love with Oliver. The colours of the passing scenery were heightened and vivid, and her heard pounded. She now had some amazing material to work with and surely would not disappoint her competitive writing group friends or, more importantly, herself.

THE MONKEY 2000

for Penny

From the window display, Howard Campbell Antiques Shop in Westgate Street, Bath, looked as if it might well have a gong. Not a bespoke antique shop, nor one that had an off-putting bell, which rang as the door opened. Carla made her way in. The shop was empty, but from the rear came the smell of cigar smoke, where a presentable, middle-aged man was having a coffee and reading the paper. The buzzer under the entrance mat caused him to appear.

"Good morning. Do feel free to have a browse. Are you looking for anything in particular?"

"A gong," Carla replied.

"I'm afraid I haven't had a gong for several months now. The authentic ones are quite difficult to come by, but there are numerous souvenir ones, which I tend to avoid. Who wants a memorabilia gong from Weston-Super-Mare? I call those sort of things collectables rather than antiques." He laughed.

The shop was stuffed with junk, and after a quick look round

Carla realised there was nothing for her there. That was until she saw the monkey, propped up between two brass candlesticks, on a small triangular pine cabinet. Victorian and threadbare, he was jointed and stuffed with sawdust, with green glass eyes and a broken red button on his waistcoat. A wire protruded from his foot. He was tagged at £40.

"Where did you get this monkey from?" Carla asked, her heart suddenly racing.

"Oh, the monkey. I found him about a fortnight ago at a boot sale. Rather charming, isn't he? He's Victorian and quite a rare find, hence the price. Obviously, not in immaculate condition in view of his age, and I wouldn't recommend him as a toy for a child. I'm quite sure that his stuffing of sawdust wouldn't comply with current Health and Safety standards. I could do ten percent off the price."

"I'll buy him."

"Will it be cash?" His breath at close quarters smelled strongly of alcohol. The transaction having taken place, Carla told him that the monkey used to belong to her as a child.

"Really? How absolutely fascinating," the man said as he wrapped the monkey in tissue paper. "That really is a coincidence. I believe we were destined to meet through the monkey. He is our 'Agent Provocateur'."

The man was dressed rather similarly to the monkey, sporting a red-spotted bow tie, checked waistcoat and tweed jacket. His brogues were highly polished and Carla felt attracted to him.

"I say, do call me Howard. I'm just about to close the shop for lunch. Would you like to join me for a quick bite? I'd love to hear the story."

Lunch was offered at Café Rouge, just around the corner, and as the rest of the day was unplanned, Carla accepted. She ordered an americano and a croque monsieur, and Howard, a Danish pastry and double brandy. She filled him in with the tale of the last childhood toy.

"Will you look out for a gong for me, Howard?"

"Of course. It would be my pleasure. Do you have a card?"

Carla produced a miniature leather briefcase from her Mulberry handbag and gave him her card.

"What a delightful card holder. Where did you find it?"

"Smythsons," came the reply.

Howard liked the sound of that. He looked at his fob watch and requested the bill.

"Oh my days. This is going to sound most ungentlemanly, Carla, but I must have left my wallet in the shop. Shall I pop back and get it?"

"No, please don't worry. Let this be my treat and I'll look forward to hearing that you've found me a gong."

"I'll certainly look out for one and be in touch, and thank you so much for lunch." They parted.

Carla Baines was rich and in the highly privileged position of having too much money. Her father had been in confectionery and invented some sort of best-selling chocolate wafer. In 1960, when she was ten, he sold his business and the family moved to southern Spain to 'live the life': cheap booze, sunshine and far from jealous neighbours. (He had been the first in their cul-de-sac to have electric doors fitted on his garage and to install a swimming pool in their back garden.) As Carla and her older sister were on the verge of outgrowing their toys, many of them had disappeared with the move. She'd been told that her beloved monkey was in one of the packing boxes, but it had never emerged and time had erased the memory. To find him some forty years later evoked emotion and vulnerability. Her parents had long-since died, both pickled in gin and olives, and she and her sister, Tanya, had fallen out over the division of their parents' property and hadn't spoken since.

As was customary on a Friday afternoon, Howard went through his till receipts for the week. He had a system: any transaction under fifty pounds provided him with his weekly lottery numbers. On a bad week, he might only get one line, but on a good week several. He wrote Carla's number of thirty-six in his notebook and took her card from his breast pocket to examine it more closely. It didn't give much away – only her name, mobile number and email address. He liked her, and needed to find a gong in order to arrange a further meeting. She was attractive, but more so, he smelled money. He thought about her quite a bit over the weekend and wondered if she was doing the same. Their friendship quickly developed in his mind beyond what it was, and he decided to ring her on Monday morning, gong or no gong. She was the perfect person to help him out with a rather unusual request. Disappointingly, his two special lottery number lines did not bear fruit that Saturday, nor his twenty lucky dips.

For her birthday treat, Carla spent Saturday having a spa day with her daughter-in-law, Lisa, and on Sunday, she treated twelve of her friends to a two-starred Michelin lunch outside Devizes to celebrate her fiftieth birthday. She took along the monkey and regaled the assembled company of the find and her encounter with Howard.

"Lisa says it's an omen, and I could do with some excitement in my life. He's very charming and well-dressed, so watch this space!"

Her friends had watched a lot of Carla's 'spaces'. She seemed oblivious to the fact that her wealth attracted all sorts of men, mostly with avaricious intentions, but they were pleased that she was happy on her milestone birthday, and a lot of vintage champagne was drunk. Three years previously, Carla's husband had died in an accident while piloting their own heliocopter, and she hadn't had a serious relationship since then.

Monday couldn't come quick enough for Howard. He had resisted Googling 'gongs for sale', as Carla could do the same, but had put out a few feelers to his local contacts. After drinking two Irish coffees at Cafe Rouge, he dialled her mobile number.

"Carla. Good morning. Howard Campbell here. How are you?"

"How nice to hear from you so soon, Howard. I can't believe you have found me a gong already?"

"No, I'm afraid not yet, but I'm on the case, as they say. I feel so badly about you buying me lunch on Friday and would like to repay the favour. Are you free today by any good chance?"

"That's a very kind invitation, Howard, and I would have loved to, but I had a significant birthday yesterday and have a hellish hangover."

"Another reason to meet and celebrate. How about later in the week? I'll take you to Bradleys, and if I find a gong by then it will be your birthday present." The favour he had in mind to ask her was worth a great deal more than a brass gong and would be worth the investment. Thursday was agreed upon, and Howard booked the best table overlooking the river for 12:30 p.m.

Every Wednesday, Carla worked at the Barnardo's charity shop in the High Street. Her father had been brought up in a Barnardo's Home in Essex. Over the years, she had provided an endless supply of designer clothes and was certainly their best donor and well-known to the manager, June, who had once approached her.

"If you have any spare time, Carla, might you consider working here? Maybe once a week? We're always looking for volunteers."

"June, I'd be delighted to. I've been wanting to do some charity work for some time. Would a Tuesday or Wednesday suit you?"

"On Wednesdays, we're really in need of cover, so that would be great."

Carla hated the stale smell of the shop and sorting through the donations – many of which were unwashed and smelling of sweat – but they had a washing machine and an ironing board and this was all part of the job. The disgusting things that people brought in: used tights, dirty shoes, sticky children's books and endless DVDs. But it took her out of her comfort zone and once she'd mastered the till, the weekly experience was always rewarding.

Carla looked stunning on Thursday in a navy, tailored suit and crisp white shirt. A bottle of house champagne awaited her in an ice-filled bucket.

"How lovely to see you again, Carla." He drew up her chair. "I'm so sorry I haven't found your gong yet, but tomorrow I'm going especially to Hungerford, where they have several antique centres with lots of stalls. Champagne?"

"Thank you, Howard." They clinked glasses and toasted her birthday.

"Why are you looking for a gong, by the way?"

"It's to be a present for a very old friend, who has his sixtieth coming up. He was Best Man at our wedding and we were joint executors. He's been a wonderful support to me. They have everything, but his wife told me that he has always wanted a gong for their massive entrance hall. They live in a beautiful house outside Chippenham called The Quarters House. Do you know it? It was one of Oliver Cromwell's shooting lodges and has a large lake with black swans and a lot of land."

"How very interesting. I must Google it. So I take it you are looking for a large gong rather than a small dinner gong? They are quite hard to come by, and can be costly, but I'm making enquiries." Howard had pricked up his ears at the word 'executors'.

Tasselled leather menus were provided and Carla ordered gravlax with blinis, followed by partridge breasts in a redcurrant coulis.

"An excellent choice, and I'll have the same, please, waiter."

In his spare time, Howard had studied books on body language in order to assist his sales, and knew that by mirroring his companion his chances were improved.

"Tell me, Carla," he enquired while refilling her glass, "I know nothing about you. What are your circumstances? Are you married?"

"I still wear my wedding ring, but my husband died in a helicopter crash three years ago. He had recently qualified as a pilot and was flying solo. It seems there was engine failure over Salisbury Plain, but the inquest was inconclusive. I have a son aged twenty-nine, who got married last year. He's an engineer at Dysons."

"Oh my God, I'm so sorry about your husband. What a terrible thing, and not very long ago." He reached for the bottle. "Are you happy to stay with champagne or would you like a bottle of red with the main course?"

Carla studied his beautifully manicured hands and fake Rolex. (She knew by the rigid ticking, rather than the smooth one.) Hands were important to her, and his reminded her of her late husband. She briefly wondered what he would be like in bed, and her stomach gave a quick rush. "No, not a bottle thank you, but maybe just a glass."

"Good idea. I'll do the same as I have to work this afternoon."

"What about you, Howard?" Carla enquired.

"Me? I'm going through rather a nasty divorce at the moment. My wife was very spoiled and difficult to live with. We couldn't have children and have been separated for about eighteen months. About ten years ago, she inherited a town house in The Royal Crescent from her parents, where we lived for eight years. They are quite a rarity as most of the houses are split up as apartments now. That's something I'd like to talk to you about."

"Oh?"

"Yes." Howard cleared his throat and topped up their glasses. "I happen to know that my wife is currently skiing. Our house is on the market with Savills, and obviously she's dealing with the sale and they don't know me. There's an important document which I'd like to retrieve from my study and I need your help."

Carla was intrigued.

"What on earth could I help you with?" she enquired.

"This is a big ask: I would like you to make an appointment with Savills to view the house. I'll come with you, as your partner/husband, and on the third half-landing after the study there's a lavatory, which I will ask to use. This sounds awful, but my plan is to ask to use the loo while you continue upstairs, and I'll get the document from the study."

Carla's life, although full, lacked excitement, and she liked the idea of this unusual request. "I'd be delighted to help you, Howard."

"Thank you so much, Carla. I really do appreciate this. The appointment needs to be made before next Wednesday, when she's back. Here's Savills' telephone number."

Their conversation took on a lighter tone over coffee, and the bill was delivered with great aplomb. Howard produced a credit card, which the waiter returned with a few minutes later.

"Sir, I'm sorry, but this card seems to have expired."

"Oh Lord, I got a new card last week, but failed to change it over. How stupid of me. This really is embarrassing."

"Don't worry, Howard. I can settle the bill." Carla produced a card from her heavily stuffed wallet.

"I feel so bad about this. You must think me a complete charlatan, but might you still consider doing the favour for me?"

"Of course, no problem. I'll ring Savills this afternoon and let you know when the appointment is."

"Thank you so much. Might I suggest that you Google the floor plan of the property, number four The Royal Crescent, in order to familiarise yourself with the layout."

"I'll do that and will call you later."

They exchanged a polite kiss outside the restaurant and went their separate ways – Carla to find a new outfit to wear for the viewing, and Howard back to the shop, where he downed a couple of large whiskies.

Being a woman, Carla was naturally curious about how Howard had lived, and indeed an insight into his wife and her taste. He had unwittingly given her the perfect opportunity, but she wasn't going to enquire what exactly it was that he was looking for.

The following Tuesday, she met Howard and a Ms Cooper from Savills at eleven o'clock outside number four The Royal Crescent. Howard was wearing a fedora and a cravat.

"Good morning, Mrs Baines. Sarah Cooper." A smartly-dressed young woman with a clipboard greeted Carla and Howard.

"Good morning. This is my husband, Richard." They all shook hands and went inside.

The house was enormous and tastefully furnished, but the decoration was rather tired. Nevertheless, his wife (or her parents) had good taste, and it was on the market for £1.2m. With nervousness and anticipation, the layout of the house went straight out of Carla's mind and she lost count of how many half landings there had been until Sarah showed them the study. She glanced at Howard, who gave a little nod.

"The drawing room is on the next floor and is a fine example of completely original Georgian features. Please, after you." Sarah gestured for them to go upstairs.

"I'm sorry, Sarah, but could I use the loo quickly?" Howard asked. "Too many coffees at my breakfast meeting this morning."

"Of course, there's one just here on the right. We'll go on up. After you, Mrs Baines."

Carla and Sarah continued upstairs, where Sarah pointed out the cornicing and working shutters. "Many of the drawing rooms in the Crescent have been divided up, and this is one of the few whole ones left. It's very special."

"Yes. It's a key feature that we are looking for as my husband and I entertain a lot of his American clients at home. They'd be massively impressed with this room. It's quite stunning." Carla attempted to keep the conversation going. "How long did you say that the house has been on the market for, Sarah?"

"About six weeks now, and we've had a fair bit of interest. It's a divorce sale."

"Oh, what a shame, but do you think that means they would be more flexible on the price? Presumably they're in quite a hurry to sell, and we're cash buyers."

Before Sarah had time to answer Howard appeared, looking quite unflustered.

"Wow! This room is something else. It seems even bigger than on the website. And what beautiful Persian rugs. Do you happen to know if carpets and curtains are included in the sale?"

"I can easily find that out and get back to you later today."

"Could you give us a moment please, Sarah?" Carla requested.

"Of course. I'll wait just outside. We still have all the bedrooms to look at."

"Did you get what you wanted?" Carla whispered, her mouth dry with anticipation, as soon as the door was shut.

"I did. Let's get out of here as soon as possible. I need a fucking drink."

Carla made all the right noises in the master bedroom.

"What an amazing bed. It must be Louis XIVth."

"Yes," Sarah replied, "everyone comments on it. Mrs Campbell's husband was in antiques and the bed is certainly going with her."

"Shame. But we're very interested, Sarah. I'll get back to you as soon as possible, and hopefully later today."

The viewing completed, they said their goodbyes outside the house. Within fifteen seconds of Sarah walking off, Howard's ex-neighbour came out of his front door.

"Howard. Good to see you, man. How are you?"

"Hello Andrew. I'm fine, thanks, and you? We've just been for coffee with some friends of Carla's at No. 98." He tried to sound nonchalant. "What have you guys been up to?"

"Oh, much the same, but I got that promotion. I think Lou might be away if you were looking for her."

"No, no, we're just passing, but really well done with that promotion. We must meet up for a beer one of these days. Sorry, Andrew, but we have to dash. Be seeing you."

"For God's sake, Carla, that was all I frigging needed. Do you think that the estate agent heard him say my name?" Howard vented.

"I don't think so, and she probably wouldn't remember that you were introduced as Richard. Also, there's no reason why, as far as she's concerned, you shouldn't bump into someone you know in The Royal Crescent. She didn't turn round anyway, but I expect your neighbour may well tell your wife that he saw you here. There's nothing we can do about that, but at least you got what we went there for."

Howard felt nauseous. "Shall we go for a drink?" He sounded downcast.

"I'm sorry, but I'm going to visit a friend in hospital now. She had a hysterectomy last week after only recently being diagnosed with cancer of the womb. Very sad, but try not to worry about bumping into that guy, Howard. When do you want me to ring Savills?"

"Maybe tomorrow, saying that we have given it a lot of serious thought."

"Sure. Let's speak soon," Carla said as she got into her BMW.

She thought about the morning's experience as she drove to The Royal United Hospital, Bath and wondered whether they had acted against the law. Surely not, if he still owned half the house and there was no forced entry. Also, what might Howard's neighbour say to his wife, and what would she think, and maybe go looking for? Would she contact Howard, and what would he say? It was all meant to be a bit of a laugh, but she had quickly become involved in a conspiracy and it made her feel uncomfortable. Uncomfortable, but still intrigued. She was now part of a soap opera and was relishing her role.

Carla entered Liz's private room, bearing chocolates and expensive bath oil.

"Liz, darling, how are you and how did it all go?"

"Lovely to see you, Carla. I'm doing well and the surgeon is pleased with my progress. I should be out by the weekend."

"Are you in pain?"

"Uncomfortable, but the pain is quite under control. Anyway, enough of that. Now I want to hear all about your birthday lunch party, which I was so sorry to miss."

"It was great fun and you were much missed, but you're behind with my news: I've met a new man!"

"No! Tell me all."

Carla filled Liz in with the events of the past eleven days.

"Not Howard Campbell? Shit, Carla. His wife, Lou, is in my pilates class and the group sometimes goes out for coffee afterwards. She's lovely. The man's a complete tosser, and a compulsive gambler and drinker. Did you know that?"

"I had my suspicions, particularly because both times we've had lunch I've had to foot the bill. But he's very charismatic and fun to be with. I like him."

"Carla, you shouldn't have been part of that plan to raid his house, but obviously I won't say anything. Did you know that he has been through all her money? She bought him an up-market antique shop in Marlborough, which went bust, and then leased him a junk shop in Westgate Street. I think he lives in a flat above the shop. He really isn't good news, and I wouldn't want you to get hurt or financially ruined for that matter."

"I hear what you say, Liz, and thanks for your concern, but there's still a bit of unfinished business to be done."

"After that business is finished, whatever it is, I'd sever all ties with him. Please be careful."

"I will, Liz. So lovely to see you, and if you want me to do any shopping or anything at all for you next week, just give me a bell."

Carla was relieved that, in view of Liz's operation, she wouldn't be going to her pilates class for a while. Their conversation had unsettled her, but not put her off. Bad luck that coincidence of her knowing Howard's wife, but it seemed they were only acquaintances, and she trusted Liz implicitly with her secret.

Howard called Carla on Friday afternoon when she was at the hairdressers.

"Carla, hi. How are you? Have you spoken to Savills yet?"

"Hi there. Yes, I rang them this morning. I put in an offer."

"What?"

"Only joking! I told them that we thought the house needed too much doing to it."

"God, you gave me a fright there. That really would be too close for comfort." Howard displayed a sense of humour failure. "You took the wind out of my sails then, Carla, but let's put all that behind us. I've found you a gong and I think you'll be really pleased with it."

"Great. How much and where from?"

"It's English, nineteenth century gothic, carved oak frame, circa 1890. In excellent condition, and the brass is about three foot in diameter. Missing its mallet, but I can easily find one. My friend in Yeovil sourced it for me and is holding it aside in his shop. In view of its condition and age it's quite expensive though. He wanted £995, but I got him down to £900. I think it's a good buy at that price."

"Fantastic, Howard. It sounds perfect. Do you remember you said it would be my birthday present?" Carla teased.

"I do, and I'd like to be a man of my word, but I did think you were looking for a dinner gong, not a Rank one. I'll tell you what though: I'll provide the mallet and collect the gong. How about that as a deal? Could I ask you to make your payment direct with Charlie? I'll give you his banking details."

This sounded like both a kosher and trustworthy arrangement.

"I'll make the payment immediately, Howard. Thanks so much. Maybe you'd like to come with me to deliver it to my friends one evening next week? I'm sure they'd like to know more of its history if you can find anything out."

"Of course. That would be fun. I shall hope to have found you the long mallet by then. Let's speak next week. I can do any evening except Wednesday."

On Sunday, Carla expected Howard to ring to confirm collection of the gong, but no call came. She found herself constantly checking her phone and felt agitated. She couldn't work out whether she fancied him or not, but something wasn't quite right. She hadn't been put off by Liz's words of warning as her father had been a bit of a gambler and a drinker too, so that sort of behaviour was quite familiar, but she resisted ringing him. Meanwhile, Howard got two hundred pounds commission in cash from Charlie, which would cover the cost of the mallet and provide him with a handsome float to go to the dogs with on Wednesday. He called Carla on Monday.

"Carla, good morning. How was your weekend? I've got the gong and it's a beauty. I'm sure your friend will be really delighted."

"Thank you so much, Howard. I've fixed for us to go for a drink with Chris and Dee-Dee on Thursday evening at six, but I don't think the gong will fit in my car. Also, the track leading to their house is full of potholes. Might we be able to go in yours?"

"Of course. I'm afraid it's a bit of a white van job, but I'll make sure it's clean for you. Do you want to come over and see the gong?"

"Howard, you're a star, but I'm going to a health farm for a couple of nights today, so will be at the shop around five on Thursday. They live just outside Chippenham and the journey takes about forty minutes."

The arrangements were made and there was nothing Carla liked better than to have a few days being pampered at a local Health Farm, where she was a regular visitor. It wasn't the sort of place where you got hosed with freezing water or had to drink watery broth or go on five mile daily runs; more of a champagne-type establishment, where the cuisine was minimal, but exquisite, and she could lounge around in her dressing gown all day, indulging in beauty treatments in between.

Thursday came soon enough and the gong was indeed impressive, but quite useless without its still-promised mallet.

"What line of business is Chris in?" Howard enquired as they set off.

"Property development, mainly in London. His buildings often win awards and he's worth an absolute packet and showing no signs of retiring. I think he's a bit of a workaholic. Dee-Dee is on the committee of several charities and keeps herself busy with that."

"Cool."

"What were you up to last night, Howard?"

"I always go to the dogs in Swindon on a Wednesday evening. It's a fun night out and more low-key than horse racing. We should go together sometime. It would be a novel experience for you."

"I used to go to the dogs in Walthamstow as a child when we lived in London. My father owned a couple of greyhounds and liked a bet. I remember he once, at my request, put a pound on a dog called Highgate Lady, as we lived in Highgate Avenue, and it came in first at 14:1, so I made fifteen quid, which was a lot of money in those days."

"Then we must go. How about next Wednesday?"

"I'd like that. Take this left, Howard, and then shortly left again. We're nearly there."

Howard assessed the house, and as they parked, he made a plan.

"Shall we leave the gong in the van and I'll go out and get it in a few minutes? Sort of a grand entrance."

"That sounds good."

Introductions were made and they had drinks in a most beautiful octagonal room, overlooking the floodlit lake. A pair of framed white kid gloves were pointed out to Howard.

"These gloves belonged to Oliver Cromwell," Chris informed him. "I expect Carla told you this house was one of his shooting lodges.

"How fascinating. Carla says you have black swans on your lake."

"Yes, we have two breeding pairs," replied Dee-Dee. "They're very friendly and take bread out of your hands, but it's a little cold to go out and demonstrate that now."

"I'm going to pop out anyway," Howard said, "as Carla has a surprise for you; a birthday present I believe." He excused himself, and in the hall pocketed a pink circular snuff box from a large collection on a circular walnut table. He knew it to be an eighteenth century Battersea Bilston enamel one with a street value of some five hundred pounds. He put it in the glove compartment of his van.

The gong, presented in bubble wrap, went down very well with Chris.

"Carla, this is ridiculously extravagant and generous of you. What a beautiful thing and just what I wanted."

"I'm sorry it's missing the original mallet, but Howard's going to find one for you."

"There will be absolutely no question of that. I'll get the mallet myself. What sort do you recommend, Howard?"

"Well, I've been looking for a twenty-four inch Paiste symphonic one. They're made in Northern Germany and would make a good match."

"I'll make a note of that. Do you know anything about the history of the gong?"

"No, I'm afraid not. It came from a probate house clearance near Yeovil and my associate bought it at auction."

"I can't thank you both enough for going to such trouble. Now, do you want to see the present I've bought for myself?"

They all followed Chris into a panelled library with a full-sized billiard table.

"Do you play snooker, Howard? Maybe we could have a quick frame now?"

"That sounds very tempting, Chris, and I'd love to, but the roads are getting icy and I think we should be on our way." He wanted to leave as quickly as possible.

"What charming people and what an amazing house. I do hope I didn't drag you away too soon, Carla, but the van isn't four-wheel drive and I don't fancy skidding. I think we'd better head straight back, but if you really do want to come to the dogs next Wednesday the meeting starts at seven thirty and goes on 'til about ten. We can eat there. We'll need to leave around six at the latest."

"Let's do that. I'll drive us and will pick you up then."

"I always take cash. The minimum bet is fifty pence, so it's not exactly the Royal Enclosure and you certainly don't need to wear a hat. It's very casual and can be cold, so dress up warmly."

It came as no surprise to Carla that no invitation to supper was issued when they got back to Bath. Besides, she was damned if she was going to pay again, especially as Howard had managed to get away with not buying the mallet either. She was going off him and rather regretted accepting his invitation to go to the dogs, but once again curiosity had got the better of her. And the need to fill her time. She withdrew seven hundred and fifty pounds, a sum which wouldn't be missed if she lost it.

The stadium on an industrial estate outside Swindon resembled a prison. A utilitarian building with tiny windows and the basement car park smelt of urine. A lino staircase took them up to the main viewing gallery – a large room with a bar and tote desk and greasy carpet tiles with plastic tables and chairs overlooking the course. A badly cracked glass door went out to the terrace by the track. But the most peculiar thing of all was that Howard had pre-booked and paid for their entry tickets, which included race cards, meal and drinks vouchers.

As the traffic was bad, they missed the first two races. Howard had prepped Carla in the car about the betting choices and recommended going for two winners or an each-way bet race rather than reverse forecasts or trios.

"I never make more than a five pound bet, usually just a pound. I study their weights, history of wins, how old they are and how often they've run," he advised Carla.

"I'm just going to go by names I like, as I did with 'Highgate Lady'."

Her first bet was five pounds on 'Slim Sid' as her grandfather had been called Sid. It won her eleven pounds. Howard had no luck with his pound on 'Turquoise Arrow', but he fared better with 'Sleekasyoulike' and netted seven pounds fifty.

"Carla, look at this. One of the dogs in four races time is called 'Speedy Gong'. It's a sign for us! I'm going to use your lucky name tip and put a fiver on him to win."

"I'll put on fifty quid."

"Wow, but it will be a good return as he's only racing for the eighth time and has no track record. The odds should be good. Shall I go and put our bets on now?"

"I'll do mine, thanks," Carla replied, with a learned caution at the thought of Howard looking after both her money and her tote slip.

When Howard was getting drinks, Carla put five hundred pounds on Speedy Gong to win.

"A monkey," said the bookie, "That's a lot of money. Good luck. As you've placed such a large bet, Madam, should the dog win, you will be paid by cheque, but it's still obviously tax-free."

"Are you getting hungry, Carla?" Howard enquired as she returned to the table. "Our food needs to be ordered from upstairs, so I'll go and do that now."

He returned with two scampi and chips in baskets and various sachets of sauces and dirty cutlery. They ate in silence, both feeling apprehensive about their bets.

'Speedy Gong' came in first, by a very short margin at odds of twelve to one. Howard was ecstatic.

"Carla. I've won sixty-five quid and you've won an incredible six hundred and fifty. This must be beginner's luck, but I did choose 'Speedy Gong', so feel that we should share both our winnings."

Carla was having none of that.

While Howard was in the gents, Carla collected her cheque from the tote desk and left. The thrill of being deceptive – and getting away with it – gave her a huge and unexpected buzz. She felt excited and drove home fast. How Howard got home was his affair.

Her friend, Liz, rang her ten days later.

"Carla, I must speak to you face to face. Can you come over now? It's about Howard. I've just bumped into his ex-wife at the supermarket."

Carla's heart sank. She hadn't heard from Howard since leaving him at the dogs, and had hoped he'd be a thing of the past.

Liz made them a coffee.

"I'm sorry to tell you this, Carla, but Howard Campbell was arrested yesterday on suspicion of theft on account of the CCTV, which his wife had recently installed in their house. He's on bail until the trial. The hearing will be at The Magistrates Court soon."

"Oh no, Liz, that means that I could be implicated too. This is really bad. What shall I do? Did you tell his wife that you knew me?"

"No, of course not, but I think you should go straight to the police and explain how you became involved. Tell them that you didn't know what he was looking for, tell them everything: how you fancied him, how it was a bit of a lark. It wasn't you who stole the whatever-it-was. He was purely using you. Did you ever find out what he was after, by the way?"

"No, I didn't even want to know; it would have involved me with too much information. I think he may have also stolen a valuable antique snuffbox from my friends' house. I defended him, but have my suspicions. I can't tell you what problems this guy's caused me. I should have stopped the friendship weeks ago, as you suggested."

Carla drove straight to the police station and gave her statement. Ten days later at Howard's trial, he pleaded guilty to theft. He was fined a thousand pounds and given a non-custodial sentence of one hundred and forty hours Community Service. Carla attended the hearing but no eye contact was made between them. As an accomplice, she was cautioned and fined five hundred pounds, but not given a criminal record.

Howard's shop was closed down shortly afterwards and the windows whitewashed.

It had been a strange, but in some ways exciting few weeks for Carla. In hindsight, she rather pitied Howard and his pathetic little scams. All he wanted was to have an easy life of no work and all play, like so many men in her world. Stealing the snuffbox had been despicable, but she'd replaced it and in an odd way, it had brought her closer to Chris and Dee-Dee. She was too hideously embarrassed to tell her son about her involvement with Howard, but was pretty sure that Tanya would never find out as it would really give her something to crow about. She wasn't worried about losing face in front of her friends as she knew too many of their skeletons.

All she had benefited from their association was finding the monkey. While much treasured, her long-lost toy was also a constant and unwanted memory of Howard Campbell.

BIBA AND BAKSHEESH 2010

for Polly

Sherborne, Monday 24th May

Patrick was disgusted. The scene and sour smell sharply reminded him of similar incidents in the dormitories of his prep school: the unsettling commotion of bright lights, matrons wielding galvanised buckets with grey, stringy mops in the middle of the night, and beds being stripped and boy and teddy bear being taken away to the luxury of the San, with the promise of a Roberts radio and hot, milky drinks at night.

Collecting Josh from his weekly judo lesson in the village hall every Monday evening was part of Patrick's routine. He usually took the dog and arrived ten or fifteen minutes before the session had finished to show support to his twelve-year-old son. That evening, it afforded him quality time for his thoughts about the text. He wasn't very practised at emotional thinking and found it more comfortable to revert mentally to his work commitments and anticipated house sales, rather than address the vexing matter in hand. He did not relish the large pool of sick in the lobby, nor the boys' excitement and curiosity. It all disturbed his routine, when he had enough to think about.

Outside the hall, whilst waiting for Josh to get changed, Patrick had the opportunity to read the text message again. After a frantic and urgent check of his raincoat pockets, his stomach lurched. He must have left his phone at home, but was fairly confident that Caroline would never touch it, as he wouldn't hers. He trapped a pebble underneath his shoe and concentrated on rotating it under the ball of his foot until the arrival of Simon Daly interrupted his preoccupation.

"Evening Patrick. What do you make of the coalition government?"

"Oh, it could be worse, but property prices are buoyant and I'm more concerned with how it will affect the housing market," was Patrick's response. He wasn't in the mood to get into predictable banter with Simon, whose confident manner irritated him.

"Did you watch the match on Saturday?" continued Simon. "What a result."

"Yes, indeed."

Patrick wondered whether Simon had ever had a Biba in his life and doubted it, but you never knew what went on in other people's marriages. He was desperate to get back home and find his phone, but Josh was, as always, nearly the last one out. They walked home companionably, with Josh regaling him with the sequence of events of the vomiting saga.

Patrick had deliberately left the dog at home in order to give himself another opportunity to get out of the house and re-read the text. The thought of it wrapped him in warmth and delicious secrecy, giving him a feeling of energy and excitement. Bailey was waiting on the doormat to greet them enthusiastically and the judo bag was dumped in the hallway. Patrick was mightily relieved to find his phone in the bowl on the hall table, which mostly contained miscellaneous items – deemed to be useful - but which never actually left the bowl: an expired pizza delivery offer, a radiator key, three golf tees, a couple of Maddie's hair ties, a coupon for discounted cosmetics at Boots and some loose change. He poured himself a beer and waited for his wife to come off the phone in the kitchen. She beckoned him to call the children for supper.

The table was laid with a small bowl of salad and a rectangular pyrex dish of thick, bubbling lasagne.

"That smells like Tom's puke," declared Josh.

"I don't think we want to know any more about that, thank you, Josh. Now eat up – you still have homework to do," Caroline told him.

Whilst pudding was being produced and the dishwasher loaded, Josh gave Maddie, his twin sister, a kick under the table and imitated throwing up into the empty salad bowl.

"I'll take Bailey out now," Patrick announced when the table was cleared.

"Come on, old chap." Bailey was lying on his side by the Aga and was reluctant to go out in the drizzle. They took off in the direction of a recreation ground behind the town library, although Patrick was very tempted to stop in at The Chequers for a drink. The idea of bumping into Simon Daly put him off, so he sat down on a wooden bench to check his mobile again while Bailey had a sniff around the municipal bins. No more texts.

Luxor, Monday 24th May

Hugh and Isobel travelled from the airport to the boat in a small air-conditioned minibus. Their guide, Menkaure, wasted no time in advising them of the local customs, particularly tipping. "Is custom to tip boat staff and guide at end of your cruise. We call it 'Baksheesh'. LE150 per person and is nice to give coach drivers a little baksheesh on trips. Maybe LE20 per couple." He spoke very fast and his intonation was unfamiliar, but they got the gist. As an Egyptologist, Hugh was familiar with the carry-on.

"Also not good to drink water from tap in your bathroom. And no ice in drinks when off boat."

The driver spoke no English and was reprimanded several times by Menkaure to maybe drive more slowly or to take a sudden cut through the backstreets. Isobel, who hated flying, was recovering from the ordeal, and the erratic driving, hooting and swerving made her feel nauseous. It was her first trip to Egypt and had taken Hugh a lot of persuading to visit for a holiday destination.

The M.S. Nile Goddess was moored down steep steps off a promenade, lined with bushes of purple bougainvillea and colourful shrubs. A couple of policemen with guns were idling around, smoking and chatting. One of them gave Isobel a lecherous look.

At first sight the boat looked rather tatty compared to the white, fibreglass, floating palaces moored nearby. She was constructed in the style of an old-fashioned paddle steamer, and her livery of cream and racing green appeared tired and dated in comparison, but Isobel concealed her initial disappointment and they crossed the thinly carpeted, roped gangplank. The reception area was cool and smelt of disinfectant. Dark red carpets were being hoovered and dimly lit corridors were crowded with overspilling dirty laundry baskets and clear sacks of empty water bottles and cabin detritus.

"Please. Welcome to Nile Goddess," said a smartly liveried young Egyptian man at the reception as he checked their travel vouchers and took possession of their passports.

"Excuse cleaning. We are late arriving to Luxor today. Please, lady and gentleman, follow me."

They were led along a corridor flanked alternately with high brass ashtrays, filled with smooth, white sand, and small fire extinguishers. Isobel took the strong smell of Dettol to mask something more unpleasant. Her main concern about the trip being an outbreak of food poisoning in the confines of the boat.

Their starboard cabin overlooked the Nile rather than the bank and had twin beds pushed together, tightly covered by a heavy, brown Moorish quilt. A slight odour of stale cigarettes lingered in the room and the window was shielded by a heavy plastic curtain with grey nets behind.

"Do open the window, Hugh, and turn down the air-conditioning. It stinks of cigarettes in here."

Hugh wrestled with the curtain arrangement to let in some

light. The smell of tobacco was soon replaced by diesel fumes and the noise of generators. One side of the cabin was crudely panelled and the rest wallpapered with cream and green stripes. The ceiling was the colour of nicotine, but it was adequate. As was customary, Hugh inspected the compact shower room to satisfy Isobel's obsession with clean en-suite facilities, and to make sure that there was absolutely no evidence of previous occupants.

"I'll unpack then," offered Isobel, as Hugh was keen to explore the boat. "Don't forget your Panama, the sun's very strong." She badly needed some time to herself and as soon as the cabin door was shut she gazed out at the smooth, olive green Nile. Small ripples by the boat carried a flotsam of orange peel, flaps of pitta bread, plastic bottles and empty cigarette and crisp packets, but the middle of the river was like a glassy mirage. Feluccas glided past, flying their Bob Marley or Che Guevera flags, their torn parchment-like sails catching the slight breeze. Palm trees and small, gaily-painted concrete dwellings on the west bank, interspersed with elegant minarets. It was all so unfamiliar and she felt a long way from Baksheesh. She sent him a text before unpacking.

Hugh returned to the cabin a few minutes later.

"Tea's being served on deck, darling. Do come up. There are a pretty rum assortment of guests, but we expected that."

A reassuringly British queue formed to be served India or China tea with creamy milk and thin slices of marbled cake and small, sweet pastries. They watched two men in a rowing boat with an iguana on a lead, leaping around and doing tricks before it retrieved LE notes of small denomination thrown down by the passengers on board.

"The things these guys do for money. Further down the Nile

they have no currency and rely totally on barter," Hugh informed Isobel. "Considering we are under six hours flying away from England, it's pretty Third World."

"I think it's enchanting, Hugh. I'm going to be too busy absorbing all the sights to read my books."

Sherborne, Tuesday 25th May

Patrick made the short walk to his office in town to open up just before nine. Both of his partners were out on viewings and he made himself a strong black coffee before checking his emails. The secretary, a hypochondriac of epic proportions, was having more blood tests for the latest something or other and not due in until lunchtime. He had no appointments in the diary, which was just as well as he was still disconcerted by the suggestions of yesterday's text. He was in unchartered waters and felt massively out of his depth. His tidy desk reflected his personality – neat, uncluttered and with everything under control. Except that, now it wasn't. He indulged himself by recalling, for the umpteenth time, when the whole thing had started.

*****

It had been a beautiful late June day the previous summer and quite a coup for the agency to have the exclusive sale of Carlton Place, an elegant six-bedroomed Regency manor house overlooking the Cole valley, near Wincanton. His clients, Hugh and Isobel Bracher, were charming and most welcoming.

"You've been very highly recommended by our friends, the Chapmans," Isobel greeted him.

"You're very kind, Mrs Bracher. I remember them well. They

had a pretty straightforward, quick sale and I think all parties were pleased. Very nice people to deal with."

"Do call me Biba, Patrick. My little sister couldn't say Isobel and her nickname for me has stuck. As I said on the phone, we're down-sizing in view of Hugh's impending retirement and want to be nearer to his grandchildren, who live outside Bradford-on-Avon."

Patrick thought it must have been a second marriage; Isobel looked about twenty years younger than Hugh and had referred to 'his' grandchildren. She was very pretty, dark-haired and petite, dressed in a knee-length flimsy floral dress. He couldn't help noticing the outline of her panties as she stood up to pour them a glass of rosé and it gave him an unexpected twinge.

"You must think us terribly decadent to be having a glass of wine before midday, Patrick, but it's so lovely to enjoy the garden and the heat while it lasts."

"Absolutely not. I would be doing exactly the same, but only the one glass for me, thank you. What an exquisite garden. Do you have a gardener?"

Hugh snorted. "You can't really call Reg a gardener, but he does the lawns and box hedges. Biba is the green-fingered one around here and does all the planting and herbaceous borders."

"It's very impressive and an excellent selling point too, at this time of year."

She smiled and caught Patrick's eye for slightly longer than was comfortable before continuing. "Patrick. We're hoping to find a town house in Bradford-on-Avon. Three or four bedrooms. Maybe you could help us with that too?"

"Of course. I'd be delighted. There are some lovely properties there, which we get on our books fairly regularly." The house phone rang and Hugh excused himself.

There was a short but highly charged silence between them – Patrick imagining her having sex with Hugh, and Biba thinking how quietly attractive he was. Just her type.

"Well, I'm sure you'd like to have a look round the house and we can do the garden if time permits. Do follow me."

In Patrick's mind the entrance hall of a large house sets the tone, and this one certainly did. It had chequered black and white floor tiles, a sweeping staircase and beautiful Georgian furniture.

The tour concluded, Patrick advised Biba that the house would command a sale price of around £1.3m. "Obviously you'll want to discuss this with your husband and, if agreeable, I'll come back later in the week to take measurements for the floor plan and photographs for the brochure. Let's hope the weather holds."

"That would be fine, Patrick. I don't know where Hugh has got to, but he's very involved with studying some ancient hieroglyphic texts which have recently been discovered. He's an Egyptologist."

"How fascinating. Please say goodbye to him from me, and thank you for your hospitality. I'll be in touch by tomorrow to arrange my next visit." They shook hands and as Patrick drove away he had the strangest feeling of the sea withdrawing and a tsunami approaching. He could recall the exact conversations of that day as if it was yesterday for it was to be the start of the most significant period in his life.

Luxor, Tuesday 25th May

Just before seven, Hugh found himself jostling at the reception with half the boat's passengers before going on an early morning trip. Everyone was under-dressed in baggy or brief shorts with comfortable trainers and baseball caps (some worn back to front). All were heavily burdened with cameras, video-recording equipment and bottles of water. Having each been issued with a greasy, laminated card with a number on, like a school children's outing, they were herded onto the gang-plank and in to the waiting coaches.

It was a long and hot morning visiting The Valley of the Kings and Queens on the west bank and the Temple of Queen Hatshepsut. Hugh was of course familiar with all of them, but had not visited since he was at Oxford, some forty years previously. His career had taken a brilliant path: he had been fortunate to get a job as a researcher under Harry James for the *Journal of Egyptian Archaeology* when he came down in 1969. In 1972, he became involved with curating the Tutankhamun Exhibition in London, again working closely with Harry James. He went on to become a Professor of Epigraphy at Oxford and lectured all over the world. The regular travelling and commitments proved a strain on his first marriage, which had been brief, but produced a son, Stephen. He'd met Biba in 1988 when lecturing at The British Museum, where she was a guide, and they had married when she became pregnant with their son, Theo, in 1994.

On returning to the boat, Biba was to be found on deck in the canopied area, chatting to a couple from Slough. The man looked Indian and his companion a blingy, loud-mouthed woman, several years his senior. She shouldn't have been wearing a bikini, let alone one with a g-string bottom.

"Oh, hello, Hugh. This is Ramesh and Babs. How was the excursion?"

"How do you do. Long and hot, but very worthwhile. Obviously nothing has changed archaeologically since 1967, but they now limit visitors in groups to the smaller chambers for health and safety. More vulnerable areas have been cordoned off to preserve them, which is a shame because some of those pillars have the most detailed and advanced hieroglyphics. I remember struggling with them at Oxford."

Ramesh and Babs listened half-heartedly, but privately thought he was from another planet and a right bore. They had come for a week of sunshine, booze, idleness and sex.

Biba was relieved to have had a late and leisurely breakfast and not to have spent the morning inspecting ancient relics. She had made it quite clear to Hugh that she wouldn't be accompanying him on any of the early morning trips, but would be interested in the local markets and restaurants.

The brass bell at reception rung for lunch at exactly one o'clock and there was a general rush to the dining room, where an enormous array of hors d'oeuvres and a cold buffet awaited. The steaming vats of pumpkin soup and lamb stew looked quite disgusting, but the choices of salads, cheeses, fish and meats were tempting. Pudding was a choice of fruits, sticky cakes or rice pudding. All tastes were catered for.

During lunch, the sound of clanging chains and raised voices heralded their departure from Luxor. The diners watched the gap between the promenade and the boat widen as The Nile Goddess started her engines and headed towards the centre of the river. Horns were sounded and Biba went back on deck, excited to be on the move. It was Dhuhr, lunchtime prayer, and was signalled by a recorded Muezzin's wailing from one the mosques. She watched the faithful make their way to pray, dressed in long white or grey robes. All men.

The Nile Goddess glided between a plain of flat, irrigated, verdant fields, where naked children splashed at the water's edge and workers tilled the land with buffalo and plough in the sweltering afternoon heat. Egrets perched on logs floating by. It was a visual symphony to Biba's eyes and she could now understand her husband's love and fascination with Egypt. She cursed herself for not accompanying Hugh before to this barren but enchanted land.

Around four o'clock they approached the lock at Esna, a deep, slimy sluice of several hundred feet long and forty feet deep. Two boats only could be accommodated at a time. Whilst they were rising from the murky depths boys in loincloths haggled on the bank.

"Ali Baba, please, please. Cigarettes, lady. Please kind lady. One cigarette, please lady, nice lady. One cigarette." Biba felt fuelled by the short opportunity to gratify the boys' request, whilst older boys threw their wares onto the deck - tablecloths, throws and sarongs – trusting that their unwanted merchandise would be returned in the short time space. She asked Babs for two cigarettes and attached them to an empty water bottle with a discarded, perished hair-tie because a weightless cigarette would never have made it. Adrenalin flooded through her with the impending act, which took on massive importance. A few other guests watched with interest and she knew she would feel a huge loss of face were the mission not to be successful. She lobbed the baksheesh to the scavenging boys. The bottle was caught by the smallest one, resulting in a scrap, whereby one of the cigarettes got broken, but still retrieved, and the little boy got the jackpot of the whole cigarette. Others scrabbled around on the dusty bank for coins, pens and lighters, and the water bottle was thrown back on deck. "Lady, lady, nice lady. Packet. Packet." And they were gone.

Sherborne, Wednesday 26th May

There had been no further texts since the one on Monday afternoon, which was both a relief and a disappointment to Patrick. He knew that contact would be limited and only through Biba in case she and Hugh were in a taxi or confined space. Again, this was foreign territory. He had never had an affair before and didn't know the rules when one party was on holiday. He loved his wife and children and knew that the situation could potentially destroy his family, but the roller coaster of clandestine excitement was irresistible.

He was on his way to measure up and photograph a dilapidated barn with some land for redevelopment near Milborne Port. The rapeseed in the surrounding fields was late in flowering and nearly over, but still aggravated his hay fever. Returning to the office in the early afternoon with streaming eyes, he made a few calls and then took the afternoon off to watch the cricket at home. For once, his secretary was in the office and unencumbered by illness, so he left her to hold the fort.

Caroline was playing tennis with a friend and it was good to have the house to himself. His thoughts returned to Biba and he went upstairs for a quick secret moment on the marital bed.

He wondered what she was doing and tried to push the contents of her text message out of his mind.

Wednesday was the only evening that Josh and Maddie didn't have after-school activities, so he wandered into town to get charcoal and some sausages and burgers for an early barbeque to give Caroline an unusual mid-week break from cooking. He toyed with the idea of buying her some flowers from the supermarket, but when he had done so before she had told him that men only gave their wives flowers if they were guilty of something (unless it was for a birthday or occasion). Perhaps they would have some special time when the children had gone to bed, but she wasn't very receptive to his advances and their sex life had dwindled over the past couple of years. This made him think about Biba again and he felt guilty and confused for both missing her and looking forward to the barbeque with his family.

While the children were doing their homework, Patrick made gin and tonics for himself and Caroline and lit the barbeque. A text vibrated on his phone, which caused him to gulp down half the drink before Caroline had started hers.

"Well, this is a first," she said sarcastically. "Whatever inspired you to do this? You're not having an affair are you?"

"Of course not, darling. For goodness sake, I took the afternoon off work because of my hay fever and thought I would give you a night off cooking." He sighed. "Why are you always so bloody suspicious?" Already the tone had been set for the evening and Patrick turned the meat with a heavy heart. He and Caroline were nearly through a bottle of Merlot by the time supper was ready.

"We must get rid of that stupid old contraption and buy a gas barbeque, Patrick, like the Dalys have. It's a complete waste of time and the children are starving."

"I don't want a gas barbeque – particularly if the Dalys have one. I can't stand that man, nor tolerate his stupid, chattering wife or their boring, socially-aspiring friends."

"For God's sake, calm down. Whatever's wrong with you? It was only a suggestion. Why are you so bloody touchy?"

The food was enjoyed, but eaten in silence. Patrick cleared away and had a swift lager from the fridge whilst getting the ice cream and bowls out. As he returned outside he heard the word 'Biba' and tried not to fall over with the tray.

"Maybe Daddy will know," he heard Caroline say. His heart raced.

"Patrick, Maddie was asking about Biba. Do you remember anything about her? I think she was Egyptian. She had an avant-garde fashion shop in Kensington High Street in the early 1970's, but by the time I was a teenager the store had gone bust."

"Why on earth should I? Never heard of her."

"Why are you asking, Maddie?" Caroline probed, a question Patrick was not going to ask.

"Some teachers were talking about her in the lunch queue today and I liked the name. Can I change my name to Biba?"

"Of course, sweetheart," said Caroline, "but only a few weeks ago you wanted to be called Jazz."

"I don't like my name. Some of the girls call me Mad Maddie at school."

The evening had been tense and disappointing and the prospect of a life of love, sex and laughter, with no family dramas, seemed thoroughly appealing to Patrick. Whilst in the bathroom he read Biba's text about her enchanting holiday and he missed her dreadfully.

Edfu, Wednesday 26th May

The boat had docked at Edfu late the evening before and Biba awoke to new scenery. It was not more than a street village, but with an impressive temple rising above the dull, half-built concrete buildings. She skipped breakfast and instead had a cappuccino on deck whilst watching the sewage being piped from the boat through large yellow hoses into waiting containers. The short promenade was stacked with sacks of cement, rubbish bags and old tyres, an ugly contrast to the colourful hibiscus and orange trees in Luxor. Hugh had gone early to visit the temple, the second largest in the country, after Karnak, and the one Hugh was most keen to visit again. The hieroglyphics had some five hundred new letters, making them challenging to read.

Babs and Ramesh were sunbathing by the small, raised pool on deck, their shared ashtray already overflowing with butts. Biba couldn't help overhearing a very pallid woman relaying her nocturnal tummy troubles. Others were complaining about silverfish in their showers and someone had found a cockroach in their wardrobe. She loved her quiet mornings on the boat and already a routine had been established. It felt like she had been there for ever and she felt stimulated by the heat, sights, sounds and smells.

A sister ship, MS Nile Gloriana, docked parallel to theirs and Biba observed that the people on board were much the same as on the Nile Goddess. She and Hugh hadn't made any friends on the boat, but that was fine.

A young, handsome male cleaner was finishing off their cabin and had made his daily different creation out of the white towels of a lotus flower on their bed.

"That is beautiful - you're so clever," Biba commented while collecting her pool bag.

"Thank you, lady. I make beautiful flower for beautiful lady. I watch you and you are very nice, kind lady. We never have one like you on boat. I think you very nice. My name Mahmet."

"Thank you, Mahmet." Biba wasn't sure if the flattery was genuine or just a prelude for the impending tip, but she liked to feel it was the former. He couldn't have been more than twenty.

Hugh returned earlier than usual and they left the boat to look around the small market and stalls on the promenade. A board by the gang-plank on the bank informed them that the boat would be departing Edfu for Aswan at one pm. The moment they were on the quayside they were bombarded with haggling vendors, who draped them in scarves, hats and leather belts.

"Good price for you. Very cheap, very cheap. See this, Sir, I give you this. Please take." A small laminated mat with a photograph of the temple was pressed into Hugh's hand.

"No thank you." They disentangled themselves from the proffered wares and headed for the cafe.

"I'm afraid it's like this everywhere on the tourist route, but they have to make a living. The trick is not to make eye contact," Hugh advised. They ordered mint tea in the grubby cafe, which was not more than a large wooden hut and had a filthy carpet of plastic turf. Local men were devouring bowls of thick, brown stew.

"Let's get back, Hugh. The mint tea is lovely, but this place is depressing."

The landing outside the restaurant on board was set up with rails of gaudy garments: tunics, Egyptian costumes and beaded headwear to sell to the punters for the forthcoming Galabeya party – the height of the cruise's entertainment. Guests were rifling through the costumes and trying them on over their swimwear.

"I think we'll give this one a miss," said Hugh until he read the flyer promising a belly dancer at nine-thirty. "Well, maybe we'll just go and have a look. Could be entertaining, but I'm definitely not going in fancy dress."

The heat of the afternoon was excessive and Hugh slept in the cabin for several hours after lunch. Biba was happy to drink in the passing green and peaceful scenery on the shaded deck and she wished that Baksheesh could share it with her. She suddenly felt guilty for not being more in touch with him, but the days had gone so quickly and been so full of new experiences, which had rather taken her mind off him. She began to doubt whether her predictable days alone at home were a large part of the cause of their relationship because she didn't actually know him very well – where he lived, his wife, his habits or anything else. Their shared times of picnics and love-making were golden, but they had never been away for the weekend together or gone to the supermarket, or been in a traffic jam, so it wasn't real. He would probably turn out to be just like any other man – lazy, sports-mad and boring. She sent him a text: 'Incredible here. Missing you. B.x'.

Sherborne, Thursday 27th May

Patrick had taken the day off as Josh and Maddie were on half term for eleven days and a trip to Longleat was planned with an early start. He liked to adhere to travel plans and timings with military precision, having had a short spell in the Army after leaving school, before deciding it wasn't for him. The route and mileage had been meticulously calculated the evening before while Caroline made packed lunches. He refused to pay over-inflated prices for sub-standard food in the on-site cafes. They were already fifteen minutes late in leaving, Caroline having got her period and in a filthy mood. The hour's drive was typically fractious, despite the usual distractions of i-spy, counting horses and spotting yellow cars, whereby the spotter could yell 'yellow car' and hit the loser before a scrap ensued.

"That's enough," Caroline shouted, "or we'll turn back."

Rather like going to Ikea, the visiting cars proceeded through the different areas in a strict, slow order. First was the monkey and gorilla enclosure. It was the children's favourite as, much to their joy, on a previous visit a large monkey with a blue bottom had jumped onto the car's bonnet and ripped one of the windscreen wipers off before chewing the rubber and and flinging it into the undergrowth. As there were notices everywhere not to leave your vehicle it couldn't be retrieved.

A small monkey landed nimbly on the windscreen, shortly before the exit.

"Oh my God. Not again, please," pleaded Patrick, but the creature merely peered in on them and settled down with its bony knees pressed against the windscreen. Josh and Maddie screamed with delight while the creature proceeded to masturbate, while looking down on his small penis unashamedly. Patrick grimaced while Caroline tried to conceal her amusement.

"Why does he do white wee-wee, Mummy?" Maddie asked her mother.

"Because it's a special magic monkey wee-wee," Caroline replied, whilst exchanging a triumphant smile with Patrick.

The magic monkey wee-wee was never forgotten, but Patrick suspected that Josh may have had an idea as he was now approaching puberty. The car remained intact and an enjoyable day was had. They got home just before seven and Patrick went to collect Bailey from a neighbour and then to The Chequers, where he had a pint and read The Telegraph. It was the first opportunity of the day to think about Biba and, as usual, his thoughts were confusing. Last night, he had seriously considered leaving his family for her, but today that didn't seem like such a good idea. Marital upsets tended to coincide with his wife's time of the month, but equilibrium always returned.

While a cold supper was being prepared, he took his newspaper out into the garden. "Aren't you having Evie for a sleepover tomorrow, Mads?" Patrick enquired while she was cleaning out the rabbit hutch. Maddie opened her eyes widely and spoke to her father as if he was a simpleton.

"Yes, Daddy, derrr... and we're going bowling too."

"I wish you wouldn't use that word. It's uneducated, rude

and has no dictionary definition. I don't fork out an arm and a leg to give you a private education to use slang like that." Maddie pouted her lips and crossed her arms.

"Perhaps you could collect Evie and Maddie from bowling around six tomorrow evening, Patrick, as I'm playing tennis, and I hope you haven't forgotten to get the euros for Josh's school trip to Normandy on Monday? Fifty should be plenty."

"Fifty? I should jolly well think so, though why he needs that much money for four days, with all meals and accommodation included, I can't imagine."

"Yes, well there are always ice creams, postcards and souvenirs to buy and he has to have emergency money."

"Whatever for? The equivalent of fifty euros – or less – was my termly pocket money at prep school."

"That was in the last century, Dad," Maddie pointed out.

"I'm going to watch the cricket and see if those idiots of ours have got their act together."

Aswan, Thursday 27th May

Hugh awoke early in Aswan and left Biba to sleep. A busy schedule was planned with back-to-back trips to The High Dam, The Unfinished Obelisk and The Temple of Philae. A larger than normal group was gathered at reception just before seven, half to go up in a hot air balloon and half to visit the dam and ancient relics. Hugh's yellow rubber wristband entitled him to free archaeological trips, whilst the purple wristband brigade denoted free drinks on board until midnight. Their wearers had not, as Hugh observed, once left the boat. He had not paid for Biba to have a purple wristband, but she had befriended Bob, the main waiter on deck, who provided free coffees and the occasional glass of wine when Hugh wasn't around.

That morning, again skipping breakfast, Bob presented Biba with her cappuccino and a chocolate 'B' on the top. Bob was definitely in the gratuity category. He was a small, cheerful man with yellow-stained teeth, a tidy moustache and pale green eyes.

"Thank you, Bob. You always look after me so well."

"Is my pleasure, lady. I have friends in England and would like to visit one day."

"Oh, really? Where?"

"Lewisham. Is near London?"

"Yes."

"Is nice there?"

"Oh yes. Very nice. You should go."

"You live near Lewisham?"

"Not really. It's close to London."

"But you always on your own, lady."

"My husband studies Egypt and we have come for him to visit all the temples."

"Okay, but no need to be on your own. My day off tomorrow. Maybe we meet in market and I buy you nice present?"

"I don't think so, Bob, but thank you."

There was no stopping these chancing guys, but it was hardly surprising; there were no women to be seen, and the few spotted from the minibus in Luxor wore full-length black robes and hijabs, looking like grim reapers. The all-male staff on the boat must have been constantly tempted by the amount of Caucasian, womanly flesh – and a lot of it on show – and presumably got lucky from time to time.

Bob changed tack. "I will tell you history of Nile – is made from tears of Goddess Isis, Goddess of love and magic, after her husband, Osiris, die five thousand years ago. This boat Nile Goddess. Is special."

"How romantic."

"Yes, very romantic. You change your mind, lovely lady, and I will look after you."

Biba went to her cabin to change into her bikini. The towel creation was a large hanging monkey, suspended from the door to the en-suite and made with the bed cover. It was horrible and gave her a fright. She went in search of Mahmet, who was hoovering a cabin a few doors away.

"Mahmet, I don't like that monkey. Please go and take it down now. It frightened me."

"My friend," Mahmet replied, "the monkey is God here, Atum. Big monkey is sun and moon God. Is valuable."

"Well, please can you take it down now and don't make it again."

Mahmet followed her back into her cabin, shut the door and dismantled the hideous creation before putting the bed cover back on.

"You like me to make other towel for you – maybe beautiful flower for beautiful lady?"

"No thank you, Mahmet. Don't worry."

Mahmet leant towards Biba conspiratorially. "You know Babs and Ramesh?"

"Of course. They're difficult to miss."

He whispered, "Every morning, every evening, they make fuck." Biba was amazed.

"Really? How do you know?"

"I listen. I hear. I know everything on this boat."

"I see."

"But Babs good lady. She give me cigarettes."

"I hope you don't listen outside my cabin, Mahmet."

"I do, lady, but there nothing to hear. Maybe we change that now?" He gestured to the bed and Biba could see an erection protruding under his tunic. She took control.

"Mahmet, you must go now. My husband will be back soon."

There was an air of excitement at supper, where most of the guests were in their regalia for the Galabeya evening. 'Diarrhoea Dorothy', as they had named her, was for once not complaining about her stomach and clad in a gaudy Egyptian costume and a beaded headdress. Babs (in a black wig) and Ramesh were

Anthony and a very overweight Cleopatra. In the upstairs, lounge the partakers were greeted with a weak, sweet green cocktail to the sound of 'Rivers of Babylon' blasting at high volume, which the guests clapped along to. It was embarrassing, but more so Biba felt unsettled. Her mother had died three years previously and it had been her favourite song and was played at her funeral. The belly dancer didn't materialise, so the guests milled about complaining, and Hugh and Biba had a gin and tonic on deck before going to bed. Biba hadn't told Hugh about the monkey towel business, nor her exchange with Mahmet, and was aware that their cabin might be earwigged.

Sherborne, Friday 28th May

As arranged, Patrick drove to Bradford-on-Avon to number seven Queens Parade, the three-storey Georgian terraced house he had found for Biba and Hugh the previous summer. He had his own key and Biba had asked him to look in. All appeared to be fine and it felt strange to be there without her, but it was absolutely not in his nature to snoop. He made himself a coffee and watered the garden. The house was in good order and they hadn't made any alterations. It was quite a comedown from Carlton Manor, but he had made two sales through the Brachers and they had, in turn, recommended him to friends, whom he had also made a sale through. It hadn't been his – or his parents' – wish to become an estate agent, but he hadn't enjoyed his short commission in the Army on account of his asthma and he had clear talent for selling houses. He enjoyed his work, although it wasn't his habit to sleep with his clients. Whilst they were clearly attracted to each other, his professionalism meant that Biba had made all the moves.

*****

They had arranged to view Queens Parade in September, while Hugh was lecturing in Paris. As Patrick was setting the alarm to leave, Biba stroked the back of his neck.

"Let's not go yet, Patrick. You know I like you, don't you?"

Patrick was taken by surprise. "I like you too, but I've a wife and young children, not to mention a mortgage, and I do love my wife. I'm also not in the habit of sleeping with my clients." He realised this sounded a bit clumsy.

"What's that got to do with it? I love Hugh too and I'm not asking you to stop loving your wife or your family or re-paying your mortgage. I'm not a bunny-boiler, Patrick, but there's something between us. Can you not feel it?" He turned and kissed her, surprising himself with his passion.

"God, Biba. What have we done? I must go now as I've a viewing in Shepton Mallet at midday." He seemed ruffled, but his reticence merely fuelled her desire.

"Don't worry, Patrick. I know you're a very careful person, but something magical has taken place between us and I don't want you to be vexed about it. At least the owners didn't walk in just now!"

"They both work full-time," he replied, formally straightening his tie in the hall mirror and checking his collar for lipstick.

"I'll call you. Another viewing would be a good opportunity to meet again as Hugh's away for another couple of days."

Patrick kissed her on the cheek and they went their separate ways. He hadn't actually got another viewing, but needed an excuse to get away quickly and process what had happened. He had gone right out of his comfort zone.

*****

Patrick set the house alarm on exactly the same spot where they had had that first kiss and drove back to the office. Over the past eight months he had grown accustomed to the devious arrangements they had to make and the necessary odd lie, both to his wife and partners at work, but the risks were exciting and made him feel alive. He recalled their first picnic by the river Cole, near Carlton Manor, where they had paddled and splashed in the cold, shallow water, green weed wrapping itself around their ankles. Biba had bought cherries and they spat the stones into the river. Biba's always went the furthest.

"You've done this before! It's not fair!" He tickled her.

"Never Baksheesh, I promise."

"Why do you call me that?"

"Because you are my tip, my gratuity, my reward in life."

"You're funny."

After lunch Patrick went to inspect a broken boiler in one of their rented properties in Sherborne. He didn't enjoy the rental aspect of the job, which was mundane and mostly left to one of his junior colleagues. Having arranged for a replacement to be installed the following week, he Googled the Nile to familiarise himself before remembering to get Josh's euros and collect the girls from bowling.

Aswan, Friday 28th May

The chat at breakfast was all about the fiasco of the Galabeya party the previous evening and how the guests had been fleeced for their costume purchases.

"Never mind, they'll come in useful for fancy dress parties," said Diarrhoea Dorothy, who was queuing up for her mixed pepper omelette, the size of a family pizza.

"I don't know how they can eat those omelettes full of fried onions for breakfast," Biba grimaced. The days were all about smells on board, starting with the cooked breakfasts, then garlic and chargrilled meat in the afternoons, mixed with constant diesel fumes. A visit to the market in Aswan was planned for the morning and the boat's rep gave everyone a briefing at reception.

"I don't recommend you eat anything from any of the food stalls and always haggle with prices. As a rough guide, you shouldn't pay more than a third to half of what is asked for, unless it's a very low-cost item. We also ask our clients not to patronise the horse-drawn carriages as they don't treat their horses well and underfeed them. Please remember to take bottled water with you."

Aswan was a dump: municipal cream-coloured housing blocks with large satellite dishes dominated the skyline, interspersed with mosques. Young men dressed in western style hung about in clusters on their mobile phones, and old, wizened men sat on grubby plastic chairs, drinking coffee and sucking on hubba-bubba pipes. There wasn't a woman to be seen. The small lanes bustled with barbers, chemists, food stalls, electrical shops and kiosks selling chilled drinks and cigarettes. Young children were selling packets of tissues and joss sticks on trays around their necks. Biba was fascinated by the colourful sacks of spices, and bought green peppercorns and saffron as presents to take home. Some foul-smelling brown, dried, pod-like spices promised 'Rocket Sex. More Good than Viagra!'

It was overcrowded, hot and airless and she felt claustrophobic. She covered her Rolex as best she could and gripped Hugh's hand, the sweat from their palms causing their fingers to slide like tectonic plates. "Let's go back now, Hugh, I'm not enjoying this."

The afternoon's entertainment was a sail by felucca around Kitchener's Island and an optional visit to the botanical gardens. Hugh persuaded Biba to join him.

"Come on darling. No ruins to see, I promise, but we won't do the gardens as there's little shelter in this heat. We must have a sail on the Nile while we're here and it's not a long trip if we don't do the gardens."

They queued to board the canopied feluccas moored further up the promenade, Hugh being the only man in a Panama hat and not wearing a football shirt or a Hawaiian one; his tailored shorts also in sharp contrast to the long, baggy ones, which seemed to be the trend.

Their captain explained how the feluccas sailed with the combination of wind and current, and had no engines. He showed off by lighting his cigarette from a passing craft and gave a brief history of Kitchener's Island. Hugh asked if he could take the tiller and navigated back to the shore, which earned him some credibility from the other passengers, who applauded him. "Give me baksheesh!" he joked as they disembarked.

After tea, the Nile Goddess departed for Luxor on their return journey, via Kom Ombo. Biba took in the passing scenery on a lounger on deck and felt guilty for not thinking more about Baksheesh. The Egyptian experience had taken her mind off him.

Small mud and brick hamlets nestled beside the river, hardly changed since Pharaonic times. Straw or animal fodder was stacked on the low roofs along with bunches of drying peppers, chillies and onions. Children played at the water's edge while their mothers washed clothes in the river with smooth, large stones, while white buffalo wallowed in the shallows. There was less cultivation than outside Luxor and the banks were fringed with palm trees, giving way to rocky escarpments. A dead donkey floated by the boat with an egret perched on its bloated body.

Dusk was falling when they docked at Kom Ombo and the guests were entertained to a diving display off a small boat. The boys, aged twelve or so, were slender and brown, with smiling, angular Nubian features. One of them shouted up to Biba: "You and me sleep, you beautiful lady. Give me money for school." Notes were thrown to the boys in empty plastic bottles.

Sherborne, Saturday 29th May

As was a weekly routine during the summer months, Patrick went to his parents to mow the lawn with Josh and his friend, Miles. He taught Josh how to start and run the mower. Not very practical himself, he could at least master that and help out. It was a question of time before his father needed to go into care and they relied on him for hospital appointments and mowing. Standards in their house were slipping and Patrick cleaned the downstairs loo with vigour. His thoughts turned to Biba and how little he had heard from her, but she would be home in two days. He was desperate to see her again. It was a different kind of love that he felt for Caroline. They had fallen into marriage like a rite of passage – their friends were all getting married – and Caroline wanted a wedding list at Peter Jones. Her proposal came to him between junctions eight and nine of the M11, after spending the weekend with newly wed friends in Norfolk.

"I want to have children, Patrick, and my parents would disapprove if we weren't married. We've been together for three years now."

"Have we really? Do I take it that you want to get married?" Patrick asked apprehensively.

"Yes. Why not. We're good together and would make beautiful children."

The arrangement was agreed on, but Patrick felt no rush of excitement. In fact, he felt quite subdued on his wedding day, and the marital sex on their honeymoon hadn't been a great success and was a bone of silent contention.

He had only a few days to consider Biba's text, but the thought sat uncomfortably and he tried to push it aside. Where would they live – in Queens Parade? And he'd never met Theo. How often would he see his children and how would it affect them? Maybe they could wait until Josh and Maddie were at university, but that was six or seven years away, which seemed like a lifetime, but at least by then he may have inherited from his parents. A lot of unanswered questions, which needed addressing.

Patrick's mother had prepared some cold ham, bread and cheese for lunch.

"Could you take me to my optician's appointment next Tuesday afternoon, darling?" she enquired over lunch. Damn, that was when he and Biba had a river picnic planned. He mentally weighed up the prospect of either lying to his mother or letting Biba down.

"I'm sorry, Mummy, but I've an important first viewing on Tuesday – a large estate – so I really don't think I can, but I'll pay for your taxi or maybe Caroline could take you if she's free. I'll ask her."

"Thank you, darling." Patrick changed the conversation. "Josh is going to Normandy with his class next week to visit the Bayeux tapestries and the war cemeteries," he informed his parents.

"Please give my respects to my fellow men," his father replied. "Your mother and I have never been able to face the war graves, although I believe it's a moving experience. I expect your grandfather fought as well, young man?" he asked Miles.

"No, I'm afraid he didn't because he had polio as a child and drove ambulances here."

"Well, we must be off now as I have to get back," said Patrick abruptly, suddenly needing some time to himself. "I'll ring you about the arrangements for Tuesday."

He regretted lying to his parents and letting them down – particularly as they were about to start paying Josh's and Maddie's day school fees at Sherborne Boys and Girls Schools. On returning home Caroline and Maddie were out and he and Josh took Bailey for a walk, trying to expunge thoughts about his deceptive behaviour towards his parents.

"Miles' mother is having a baby, Dad. Did you know?" Josh asked.

"No, I don't think I did. How nice."

"You and Mummy wouldn't have another baby would you?"

"No, Josh. Definitely not. You needn't worry about that, old chap." And that wasn't a lie.

Kom Ombo, Saturday 29th May

Hugh persuaded Biba to accompany him on the early morning tour to the Temple.

"It's amazing, darling. Kom Ombo means mountain of gold and is the Temple of the Crocodile God. It was also an early centre of medicine and fertility research. You can't miss it."

Biba would have preferred to have a quiet morning on deck, but she agreed as it was only a walk from the boat and didn't involve being herded around in coaches like mountain goats. Most of the other guests went to visit a Nubian village. The temple's guide spoke good English, explaining fascinating facts:

"Pregnancy testing methods existed four thousand, eight hundred years ago. Frog injected with lady's urine and after time, if frog's belly swells she pregnant. Then, to detect sex of child, if barley grow in jug of urine is boy, and if wheat grow is girl. To tell when lady is fertile, bulb of garlic inserted into woman and when her breath smell is ready."

They were shown hieroglyphics depicting medical instruments – ventouse, scissors, needles, string and circumcision tools.

The guide continued. "Then there is Sobek, the Crocodile God. Pharoah selected a crocodile to make it into a God for one year so it wouldn't eat people. Then he slayed and mummified it. This is the sarcophagus of that crocodile."

The trip had been very interesting, but Biba needed to have some time alone. Being Saturday, it was 'off limits' to text Baksheesh and she regretted not doing so the day before. Her thoughts turned to Theo, as there was generally a match to go to at weekends. He was very sporty, but she hated watching the matches on the freezing touchline and socialising with the other aspirational mothers. They were a competitive lot and all dressed in a safe uniform of navy blue trousers, puffa jackets, Hunter wellies – or loafers with gold chains on – and Cabouchon jewellery. They chatted about people they knew or their sons' achievements or husbands' jobs. Biba couldn't be less interested and lacked their social ambition and natural ability to be one of the crowd.

Bob gave her a coffee on deck and she watched the other boats come and go on the short quay, the inky water carrying oil slicks. Staff lazed at the rear of their boats, observing the regular calls to prayer, when they would repeatedly genuflect eastwards on their knees on narrow, soiled mats.

Mehmet's creation of the day was a towel crocodile, wearing Hugh's reading glasses, and it made her smile.

At lunchtime they departed for Esna lock, which was busier than on their outgoing journey, being earlier in the day. Men attached their feluccas to the boat and threw their wares up on board. It was fatal to make eye contact.

"Nice tits, lady," they said to Babs. "Lady, lady. Good price. Here, lady. Beautiful cloth. Good price from me."

A group of young men and boys got into a crude conversation with two teenage girls on the boat, who were scantily clad in miniscule bikinis.

"You have big pussy?" they asked, "what colour the hair? Big breasts? Yes! You want one metre? Him one metre and a half. Look!" He laughed and pointed to a boy with dark, kohl eyes, whose metre and a half protruded unashamedly underneath his robe.

"You come now. Five minutes with me. I promise good. Five minutes, just five minutes. Come now, we have time."

The direct and suggestive banter provided good theatre for the other guests and was received by the girls with a mixture of humour and prudism, but their mother seemed embarrassed.

"This is better than Eastenders," someone remarked.

Something Hugh had eaten at lunch had disagreed with him and he retired to their cabin. "I think I'll give supper a miss tonight, darling. Gippy tummy, but that was to be expected."

Biba shared their table with an American man, who had joined the boat at Aswan and was, as her late father used to say, 'on good terms with himself'. He was already on his second prawn cocktail and a messy eater.

"Hi. I'm Morgan. And you are?" his mouth full of food.

"I'm Biba. How do you do."

"That's a nice name. Hey, you know that head waiter, who looks like a king cobra? He gave me bad service last night and I'm gonna show him who's boss around here and bait him tonight."

"Why?"

"Because I don't like his attitude. I'm not used to waiters who are sloppy and rude."

"You have to remember this is a Nile cruise, not a transatlantic one. The standards are different."

"Standards are standards, Biba, and what difference does that make? The guy's in service, isn't he?" He snapped his fingers. "Hey waiter, come here." After wiping the surplus food from his mouth, he continued as the head waiter hovered over him.

"You know those little bottles of shampoo and body wash in my bathroom? May I take them home with me as I don't think I'm gonna finish them up."

The waiter looked perplexed. "Shampoo? I no understand. You want shampoo?" The king cobra recoiled.

"Now, you listen again and you listen good: That stuff you wash your hair with – we call it shampoo where I come from. May I take it home with me? You understand now?" The king cobra summoned a weasel-faced waiter, shrugged and walked off.

Whilst their command of English was limited to choices of food, wine and menus, it was understood that the American was making fun of them.

"Now, that was funny. Serve the asshole right."

Biba was in no doubt who the asshole was.

Sherborne, Sunday 30th May

Caroline was preparing for a lunch party when Patrick returned from getting the papers. She was prone to being tetchy before entertaining.

"Please can you set the table outside and don't forget to give me Josh's euros as I must pack for him today."

"I'll get them now." He couldn't find his jacket in the hall or upstairs and knew this would cause a row.

"I must have left my wallet in my jacket at my parents yesterday. Shit."

"How did you pay for the papers?" Caroline snapped.

"With loose change from the hall bowl."

"God, you are useless. It was the one thing I asked you to do and you cock it up. You'd better go and get it after everyone's gone."

"I'm not going over there this afternoon and not be able to have a few drinks. I do enough driving. You can get it when you take Mum to the optician's on Tuesday."

"When I what?"

"Oh, forgot to ask you if you could take her for an optician's appointment on Tuesday afternoon as I can't."

"What else did you forget? What's wrong with you, Patrick?

You seem to be going a bit soft in the head. And no, I cannot take your mother to the optician's on Tuesday as I'm playing tennis with Sarah after lunch. You can bloody well take her and cancel whatever important thing you have to do."

"I can't. It's a viewing for a big estate." Patrick instantly regretted telling the lie in case she probed him for more information. "You're always playing tennis with Sarah, so that can easily be cancelled."

"Absolutely not. James or Richard will have to do the viewing then."

"It has been decided that I'll do it."

"Well, good luck to them for dealing with a half-wit, and what about the euros? There's nowhere to get them today."

"I'll give one of the teachers forty quid and ask them to change it for him on the ferry," Patrick suggested, "and I'll order a taxi for Mum."

"What will they think of us, Patrick. Just imagine if every parent asked them to do that. Jesus."

"Oh, for God's sake, Caroline, chill out. It's a small mistake and not the end of the world. Nothing bad has happened."

"Can you please just go and lay the table outside for ten and can you change that old shirt as it's very worn at the collar."

"For ten?"

"Yes, ten, with the children. I've also invited the Dalys, last minute."

"You haven't, have you? You know I can't stand that man and his wife's so boring."

"Well, I like them and the boys get on well. Josh would feel left out otherwise as Tim and Sarah are bringing Evie."

There was nothing more to be said on any subject, so Patrick went upstairs to change.

Simon was chatting to Caroline in the kitchen when he came back down.

"Morning, Patrick," said Simon, proffering a bottle: "Some Beaujolais sperm for you."

"Sorry?"

"My little joke. It's actually rather a cheeky little number and fourteen per cent proof. 2004, a good year. Might be an idea to take the cork out now to let it breathe."

Patrick was well aware why corks needed removing from bottles and had intended to serve his own choice of red wine. He also had some notion that it was rude to drink the wine that your guests had brought unless you were still at university.

"Thank you, Simon. Where's Elspeth?"

"Afraid she's got a migraine, so it's just me and Jack. Came on this morning."

"Sorry to hear that. Come through to the garden with your drink."

Simon downed three beers in quick succession and then got onto the red wine.

"What's this we're drinking, Patrick?" he asked while examining the bottle.

"Mmm. Shiraz. I was rather looking forward to a bit of the old Beaujolais."

Patrick felt his chest tighten.

"Would you like me to get it for you?," he asked, feeling like Basil Fawlty, and that he might actually crack open the bottle on Simon's head.

"Yes, I would actually, but only if you uncorked it when I arrived as it needs that breathing time, being an old wine. Well, maybe open it anyway for later and I'll start on the Shiraz."

Patrick couldn't believe his arrogance and rudeness, but went into the kitchen to open the wretched wine and take stock. So much for happy family Sundays, but he had Tuesday to look forward to. He wondered why on earth Caroline had invited Simon Daly. He always took over everything.

The conversation over lunch was predictably about schools, exams, results and sport. Sarah and Tim hardly got a word in edgeways and Caroline was drinking like a fish.

"How are you going to manage the fees for the twins at Sherborne, Patrick?" Simon enquired. How he knew that Josh had got in to Sherborne was another matter as they'd only recently heard themselves.

"Not that it's your business, Simon, but having a scholarship helps." He suddenly felt angry and in need of claiming his territory.

"Darling, don't be silly and proud," Caroline said to Patrick in front of everyone. "Patrick's parents are helping us – there's no shame in it. They're so generous and of course we're really grateful."

Patrick flipped. "If they're so lovely and generous enough to educate their grandchildren, why can't you cancel Tuesday's tennis with Sarah and take my mother to the optician's then?"

"Oh Lord," Sarah interrupted. "I don't think we can be playing tennis on Tuesday as it's my birthday and Tim and I are going up to London. Sorry about that."

Caroline blushed, "I thought we were, but must have written the wrong Tuesday in my diary. Doesn't matter at all and it means I can take Anne to her appointment."

Simon started on the Beaujolais and didn't pass it round. He made fleeting eye contact with Caroline, who also looked pissed.

"It's nearly four. I'll make some coffee." Patrick resumed his hosting duties and hoped that the lot of them would soon bugger off. When he returned, the children were playing badminton and the bottle of Beaujolais was nearly empty.

"Listen guys," said Simon quietly, swilling the wine around his glass, "I may as well tell you before you hear it from someone else. Elspeth and I are splitting up. Well, to be more precise, she's left me."

"I'm so sorry," Sarah said. "Is anyone else involved?"

"Yes, well, no. Not any more. It's all rather a mess and she's going to stay with friends in London for half term, with Jack of course. She's collecting him tonight."

The tone of the lunch took a sombre turn and the drop in Simon's mood seemed to affect everyone. He continued:

"I'm going to have to find somewhere to rent as we want Jack to remain at school and disrupt his life as little as possible. Perhaps you can help me with that, Patrick?"

"Of course. Come and see me tomorrow if you want."

Sarah and Tim got up to leave. She put her hand on Simon's shoulder. "If there's anything at all we can do to help with Jack, you only have to ask."

"Thanks."

"That was a barrel of laughs," Patrick said as he loaded the dishwasher. I don't ever want that man to set foot in my house again." But his protestations fell on deaf ears; Caroline had gone up to bed.

Luxor, Sunday 30th May

They awoke in Luxor, having docked during the night, and Hugh was feeling well enough to go on the morning's excursion to the Temple of Karnak after breakfasting on dry toast.

"Are you sure you'll be OK, Hugh? There won't be any loos there and don't forget your Panama."

"There will be loos and I'll be fine. I've taken some Imodium and I don't want to miss the largest temple in Egypt."

After the complimentary cappuccino from Bob, Biba made sure she didn't sit anywhere near the ghastly American. His voice travelled and she could hear him banging on about something. When she went to her cabin, Mahmet was cleaning in the bathroom with the door shut, and on their bed the white towels spelled 'I ♥ U', with a red rose laid on top. She was just changing in to her bikini when Mahmet appeared. She covered herself with one of the towels.

"What are you doing in here, Mahmet?"

"I clean your bathroom. You like my towels, lady?"

"Yes, but you must go. Now."

"I no want go. I love you. I think of you every moment and I want you make fuck now. Your husband not here."

"Don't be ridiculous. Please go now."

"In my country, when I meet lady I have to marry her. I no allowed girlfriends before I marry, but how I meet girl to marry when I work on ship? My father beat me. My mother his fourth wife. She Spanish and I no see my mother since I was six years. She leave without me. It shame for my father that I am different nationality to my brothers and sisters. Maybe I come to England and you help me? I work for you."

"That's awful, Mahmet, but I can't help you. I do understand how it is to love someone, but what you have is not real love for me, just an infatuation." She took two hundred LE out of her wallet.

"I no want your money." He left the cabin like a faithful dog that'd been kicked by his owner.

Biba was upset by the episode and she felt for Mahmet's loneliness and predicament. She unravelled the towels and pressed the rose between tissues in her book. She decided to visit the little shop on board, which sold souvenirs, postcards, pens, jewellery and basic chemist stuff. A short, bearded man behind the display counter was weighing gold chains and putting them into small plastic envelopes.

"Good morning, Madam. My name is George. Nice to see you. You want to buy some gold? Gold is cheap now and I will do you a very good price. May I get you a glass of mint tea?"

"No thank you."

"Maybe a cartouche on a gold necklace? He explained the meaning of some of the hieroglyphic symbols from a tatty chart and how the letters of your name determined your character. "What is your name and I will tell you." He gestured for Biba to sit down on the rather out of place pink velvet boudoir chair and gave her a scrap of paper. Biba found the concept fascinating and could suddenly understand Hugh's love of hieroglyphics. She wrote it down.

"It's Biba – B.I.B.A."

"You are fair and kind, and a person of truth. The symbol of 'B', which you have twice, is a leg and means a courageous character and a brave personality and spirit. The 'I' is two dashes and represents good luck. And the 'A' a powerful eagle bird and is a sign of divine power, good taste and good personality."

He produced a selection of plain cartouches on a cardboard tray and Biba impulsively chose a more chunky eighteen carat gold one, his relative underselling and air-conditioned shop being more effective than the blatant hassle of the street vendors. It felt good to buy something for herself.

"It's a good choice, Biba. You have short name so can have more heavy gold. I'll get it engraved in the town and it will be ready for you at five o'clock. If you like more heavy chain I can give you good discount." Biba chose a box-like chain and paid him with her credit card.

Hugh returned tired from the trip, skipped lunch and lay down on their bed.

"Everyone's talking about a sound and light show at Temple of Luxor tonight, and supper's an hour earlier. Would you like to go? I don't really fancy it myself – all those crowds and flashing lights and being herded about in the crowds."

"Me neither."

"As we haven't had great food this week, shall we spoil ourselves and go for dinner at the Winter Gardens instead? It's Luxor's equivalent of The Ritz or The Savoy."

"That sounds a lovely idea, Hugh. Are you up for a rich meal though?"

"I'll be fine. There will be an à la carte international menu, and it's a beautiful old hotel in formal, landscaped gardens."

"I've bought myself a little present, which I need to go and collect soon and will wear tonight."

"Oh? Have you been into Luxor today?"

"No, just to the little kiosk on board. You'll be amused by it."

The Winter Gardens was opulent and grand, but promised more than it delivered. Hugh, in an open-necked shirt, was offered an ill-fitting jacket and greasy tie in order to eat in the dining room. They had half a bottle of champagne and a bowl of juicy lemon olives on the terrace and walked round the gardens before being ushered into the dining room. As soon as they were seated, the maitre d' informed Hugh that he could remove his jacket. The hotel seemed to belong to a forgotten age and the other diners, all in their seventies plus and most of them English, ate in silence or in hushed tones.

Hugh was pleased that Biba had formed an interest in hieroglyphics and admired the cartouche. "It looks good on your tanned skin, darling, but I'm not sure how well it will travel. Rather like bringing a bottle of Pernod back to England from France and it never being drunk." The spicy crab and avocado terrine was a good choice for their starter, but Biba's salmon was floating in a pool of rich, congealed, meaty gravy, with tinned peas and overcooked new potatoes. Hugh's plaice was passable, but didn't smell that fresh. Both dishes were ceremoniously revealed from under silver domes by two waiters with perfect precision.

"Hugh, this is disgusting. I can't eat it." She ordered another crab and avocado terrine. They were tired and took a taxi back to the boat for their last night.

Sherborne, Monday 31st May

Patrick's diary was quite free on Monday, which was a relief. He'd been quite unsettled about Sunday's lunch party and had picked up on the subtleties. It occurred to him that Caroline and Simon might be having an affair, and he was ruffled. The weather was changing and didn't look promising for the planned picnic on Tuesday. The week had been shitty and the prospect of living with the love of his life seemed easy and possible after the turbulent weekend. He had come to dislike Caroline and her selfishness, and imagined a harmonious life with Biba of sex, love, understanding and fun. The Test Match had finished, with England beating Bangladesh by eight wickets, which put him in a generous mood. On his way to buy a sandwich and newspaper at lunch time, an Egyptian Ankh cross caught his eye in a jewellers' window on the high street. It would make a wonderful present for Biba to welcome her back and he had never bought her any jewellery – or indeed anything. Rather beyond his means at seventy five pounds, he inspected the small, gold Egyptian cross while the shopkeeper explained that it was a sign of life and unity, and the eye of Horus, representing two different kingdoms – the lower: delta, and the upper: man. He liked the sound of that and knew that Biba would too.

"It's second-hand," the man explained, "and I don't see them very often. In fact I haven't had one for several years. I could throw in a nine carat gold chain for an extra twenty five pounds."

"That will be fine. Thank you." He couldn't very well give the Ankh without a chain.

As the gift was being wrapped, who should come into the shop but Caroline.

"What are you doing here?" she asked her husband accusingly.

"I could ask you the same question," he replied.

"I'm collecting my ring, which lost one of its diamonds, but it's only being replaced by a zirconia, so don't worry. It's not going to be expensive. What have you bought?"

Patrick had become sharper at thinking quickly. He lowered his voice, "I've bought you a present to make up for yesterday and to say sorry that I was such a grump at lunch." He didn't wish to go into more detail in front of the shopkeeper, who had a shrewd idea what was going on.

"What a lovely thought, and I'm sorry for being so snappy too. Can I open it now?"

"No. Let's wait until this evening as I've got to get back to work. Gail is off again on some new medical investigation." As the card payment was being made, Caroline noticed the sum involved on the card machine.

"Josh got off safely and there was no problem about getting his euros," Patrick reassured her. "See you later."

He had got away with it, but only just, and returned to the shop a few hours later to find something of equivalent price for Caroline. It had been a costly business.

"Hello sir, I thought you'd be back," the shopkeeper greeted Patrick with a smug smile. "I've got some pretty citrine and gold drop earrings for the same price. Are your wife's ears pierced?"

"Yes they are. I'll take them."

"I thought you would, sir, and I presume you'll be paying cash this time so as not to have duplicate receipts?"

"Yes."

Being careful not to get the presents mixed up, he hid the Ankh underneath some papers in the bottom drawer of his desk. Gratifyingly, the Telegraph reported that there wouldn't be a better time to sell your home. The significant election had caused disruption to the spring housing market and it was predicted that there would only be a few weeks for sellers to get the best prices for their houses before the market would swing in favour of buyers. Conversely, it also said that the Conservative-led government, although popular with estate agents, may indirectly provoke a market downturn. They always had to cover every eventuality.

Caroline had bought fillet steaks for supper and was in a bright mood when Patrick got home. This made a welcome change and was surely due to the impending present. The house was unusually quiet without the children.

"Where's Maddie?" Patrick enquired.

"She's gone to Evie's for a sleepover. We're all alone." She gave him a kiss.

Patrick couldn't remember a night without both the children at home and it felt strange.

"We're having fillet steaks and chips for supper – your favourite." She poured him a glass of red wine.

"It's a shame that so-and-so insisted on opening his Beaujolais yesterday. It would have been excellent with the steak. So rude," Patrick grumbled.

"Let's forget about that, and I seem to recall that there's a little present for me?"

Patrick produced the small gift bag, carrying the earrings.

"Darling, they're beautiful. Thank you. Are they citrines?"

"I believe so."

"I'm going to put them on right now – and I've also bought some new underwear to mark our first evening alone for so long. Shall we take an early bed tonight?"

Patrick couldn't think of a worse proposition.

Luxor, Monday 31st May

Suitcases were lined up in reception for the morning's departing guests. Some were going on to Hurghada by coach for another week and others to take the midday flight to Manchester. Hugh and Biba's flight wasn't until seven o'clock, so they had the morning and early afternoon to enjoy their last day. Biba couldn't believe how quickly the week had gone – being on the boat was timeless and the experiences incredible. She was sad to leave and also surprised that she hadn't missed Baksheesh as much as expected. The sending of the text had perhaps been a mistake.

As there were no activities planned for their last day, Biba requested that they visit the market. "I know they're not our favourite places, but I would like to find a rug for the small spare room." Hugh gave in.

The market was a short taxi ride away and much larger than the one at Aswan. Stacked rolls of coloured fabrics and towers of fresh vegetables and spices alternated with souvenir and confectionery shops, all selling the same merchandise: turquoise scarabs, onyx pyramids, keyrings and so on. Biba would have liked to inspect the fabrics, but could see that Hugh was becoming impatient. Gaudy and unfamiliar sweets were displayed in plastic bags, and the strong smell of raw meat didn't prepare them for a severed cow's head on the pavement outside a butcher's shop, its blood congealed in the dust.

"Please can we go, Biba. Let's forget about the rug. It would be a pain to take home and there's a good rug shop in Marlborough. We don't need any more rugs anyway, now we're down-sizing."

They headed back to the main square, Biba having purchased two small rubber bendy camels for Hugh's grandchildren.

Despite the rep's advice, Biba pleaded with Hugh to take a horse-drawn taxi back to the boat. Mule-like, bony black creatures and their blingy carriages were lined up in the square. Flies buzzed around their faces and weeping eyes. Charms and bunting dangled from their fringed canopies over the carriage. A fixed priced was agreed on with the driver.

"Please – come. My horse Egyptian Ferrari, he called Jimmy." They quickly took off, dodging the oncoming traffic and overtaking coaches on the busy road. It was nerve-wracking, but the blinkered horses showed no fear and they were soon back at the boat.

An early lunch was served to the diminished group of guests on only three tables, and they found themselves sitting with Morgan.

"Waiter, more croutons," he drawled, clicking his fingers.

The weasel-faced waiter nearly exploded. "They for soup, not for eat," he spat back.

"If I want croutons, I want croutons – get it?"

More croutons were eventually produced when the soup was finished.

"Jesus, I won't be doing this again," Morgan announced.

"You have to understand their culture, Morgan," Hugh explained. "It's very different from ours."

"Culture, my ass; they're rude and lazy. I don't tolerate sloppy behaviour – not from Egyptians, not from no one. I'll be pleased to get back to civilisation in New York."

"As we don't need to leave for a few hours, do you mind if I go out on a felucca for half an hour, darling?" Hugh asked Biba.

"Of course not. I'll go and pack. Remember your hat."

Hugh made the short walk to where the boats were moored, down a steep embankment of breezeblocks and rubbish. The boatmen were playing some sort of game with dice on one of the boats.

"You want sail, sir? Is two hundred LE for you. I take money now. Trip half hour to one hour. You English?"

"Yes," said Hugh, as the man untied the ropes and offered him a cigarette. "No thank you."

"We can go to west bank, see Temple of Karnak. Very beautiful."

The felucca effortlessly glided across the river, the boat man waving to friends on other boats. He pointed out some young boys in a rowing boat bashing the water with long poles.

"You see that, sir? They fish for mullet."

"What are they doing?" enquired Hugh.

"It attract the fish."

"I see." Although he didn't see at all.

"You think I good sailor?"

"Oh yes, very good."

"You think I strong man?"

"Oh yes." Hugh wasn't sure where the curious conversation was leading.

"I can do with man or woman. You want come down in cabin for some tea?"

"No thank you," said Hugh, who was looking forward to being back on terra firma.

"No problem, sir."

After finishing packing, Biba went up on deck to have a mint tea. Babs and Ramesh were drinking lagers with a few others and talking loudly. Babs sounded a bit drunk.

"Boy, can I recommend that Rocket Sex bark. It tastes revolting, but Ramesh had it up for hours last night!" It wasn't really that funny, but everyone laughed. Biba couldn't resist uncharacteristically joining in the conversation.

"I understand you and Ramesh don't need Rocket Sex."

"How d'you know that, you posh pervert," came the acidly quick reply.

"The towel man told me. I expect he told everyone."

Her outrageous remarks ended the conversation and Biba walked off, her head held high.

"Fucking posh bitch. Who does she think she is?"

Hugh and Biba were recounting their stories to each other while waiting for their minibus to the airport: "My God, those people, they're sex-mad," said Hugh.

"I know what you mean, but do you know what? I've really fallen in love with Egypt and I'm going to learn hieroglyphics. This holiday has really inspired me and given me a new interest. I need something like that in my life: A real interest."

ACKNOWLEDGEMENTS

I would like to thank Ted for his unfailing patience with my writing and love affair (not) with my computer.

Also Laurie and Jenny Andrews, Roddy Bloomfield, Suzie Dean, Patrick Findlater, Jade Hext, Robin Lodge, Sam MacDonald, Schuyler Pratt, Rose Ruggles-Brise, Lee Sharp and Tessa Watkins for their time, help and support.

Also my children, Max and Polly, in the hope that they won't be too embarrassed by the (moderate and infrequent) references to sex!

Most of my individual dedications have provided me with the inspiration to write the stories, so my thanks also to Alan, Alba, Bernard, Margaret, Penny and Sam.

And to my sisters, Rosie and Bunny, for their consistent love and encouragement.

Finally to Katie Isbester and her team at Clapham Publishing Services for putting up with my technophobic disabilities and who made it all possible, with efficiency, patience and ease.

Thank you all.

ABOUT THE AUTHOR

Nettie Firman lives and writes in Essex with her four dachshunds. She is an artist and this is her first publication.

If you want to contact Nettie, or purchase a copy of this book, she can be reached by email at:

nettiefirman@btinternet.com

Lightning Source UK Ltd.
Milton Keynes UK
UKHW011702290620
365747UK00006B/191